LADY EUGENIA'S HOLIDAY

LADY EUGENIA'S HOLIDAY

•

Shirley Marks

AVALON BOOKS
NEW YORK

Published by Thomas Bouregy & Co., Inc.
160 Madison Avenue, New York, NY 10016

Library of Congress Cataloging-in-Publication Data

Marks, Shirley.
    Lady Eugenia's holiday / Shirley Marks.
        p. cm.
    ISBN 978-0-8034-9986-7
    1. Aristocracy (Social class)—England—Fiction.
I. Title.
    PS3613.A7655L33 2009
    813'.6—dc22

                                        2009024265

PRINTED IN THE UNITED STATES OF AMERICA
ON ACID-FREE PAPER
BY HADDON CRAFTSMEN, BLOOMSBURG, PENNSYLVANIA

To Heidi and Ancilla for their inspiration

. . .

To Kim and my darling husband for their time

Chapter One

It occurred to Lady Eugenia Abbott that had she
not taken her aunt Rose's offer, she would have been
the one left at home, again.

Had Eugenia not refused to accompany her little
sister Marguerite and her governess, Mrs. Moss, to
the village that very morning, and had she not returned from her short walk at that precise time, Eugenia would have missed her elderly relative altogether.

"Whatever are you doing here, Auntie? You are
nearly a fortnight early for your visit." It had been over
a year since Eugenia had seen her great-aunt and had
not expected her for another month. "Mama and Papa
have not returned from Town yet."

"Yes, dear, I know all about that." Aunt Rose
stripped off her gloves and marched past Eugenia,

directly into the green parlor. "Your mother has already informed me of their delay. I have taken advantage of the situation and suggested you accompany me on my excursion to Brighton. You may have been denied the delights of London but I daresay you shall be pleased with your share of entertainment and parties where we are headed."

"Am I really to go with you, then?" Eugenia nearly fainted dead away at the good news. At last she was to have a chance to enjoy herself as Frances had.

"If you can manage to be ready in time." Aunt Rose gazed wide and winked, suggesting that her niece make haste. "And," she added, "I would like to leave in no more than an hour's time."

Eugenia shot to her feet, uncertain of what action she should take next, and then moved toward the doorway. "Will you not remain long enough to see Marguerite?" Using her younger sister's absence to keep her aunt a few more minutes at Langford Hall had been her first thought. "She and Mrs. Moss are due back from the village at any moment."

"I'm afraid that cannot be helped, dear. I believe there are fifty-seven minutes remaining of your hour."

"Mrs. Peterson!" Eugenia called down the corridor for the housekeeper, who rushed down the hall at an amazing speed for someone her age. "Please, Auntie, you must be tired from your travels. Why don't you have a cup of tea and sit while I have my things packed."

"Sit? All I've done is sit!" she remarked rather sharply. "However, tea sounds splendid. I believe I shall . . . if the staff can manage. I am sorry to drop in like this—unexpected visitors are always unpleasant."

"Not you, Auntie, never." Eugenia motioned to the housekeeper, hoping she'd join in the subterfuge to keep her aunt occupied. "Mrs. Peterson, would you be so kind as to see my Aunt Rose to the breakfast room?"

"At once," Mrs. Peterson replied. The housekeeper whispered to Eugenia, "I believe Cook is pulling some of your aunt's favorite fruit tarts out of the oven just now."

"Serve her some of those as well. I'm sure the fruit tarts will detain her for an extra half hour."

"Near an extra hour, I'd say," Mrs. Peterson amended, making Eugenia feel even more hopeful that she could be ready before her aunt's departure.

Eugenia dashed upstairs and ordered her abigail Marianne to pack for a stay in Brighton. After changing into her blue traveling gown, Eugenia rejoined Aunt Rose in the breakfast room.

"Ah, yes. Here you are—I have just finished. Now we can be on our way," Aunt Rose announced and popped the last bite of fruit tart into her mouth when Eugenia stepped into the room. "They were absolutely splendid, as always."

Three tarts and an entire pot of tea in total were consumed while Aunt Rose waited for her grandniece. To remain in her aunt's good graces, Eugenia had several tarts wrapped to bring along on their journey.

Aunt Rose laid her napkin on the table and collected her gloves and reticule. "It is most unfortunate you were denied your come-out, of course it was through no fault of your own." She led the way down the hall and into the foyer. "I am told you shall make your bows this fall."

What could Frances do after her near-year long engagement had come to an end? Eugenia's Town plans had already been made but neither she nor her parents wished for both daughters to be on the marriage mart at the same time.

Eugenia had purposely kept her expectations, and her disappointment at relinquishing her Season, to herself, never allowing any hint of her true feelings.

"I grant you that Brighton is not as exciting as London—" Aunt Rose paused at the open front door and observed Eugenia's trunks being loaded onto the transport. "But I'm sure we can manage to amuse ourselves—and keep out of trouble."

Trouble? What possible trouble could they manage at a bucolic seaside resort?

Not ten minutes after boarding the carriage, Aunt Rose turned to Eugenia to ask, "Has Frances written you of her young man? What do you know of her match?"

Frances had corresponded with her sister. However she had not been forthcoming regarding her fiancé. Eugenia hadn't learned much. "I know she is to marry Sir Russell Crawford and she does, by her account, find him . . ."

"Tolerable?"

"Oh, no, much more than that . . . she finds him more than acceptable." Eugenia considered if it was appropriate to add her personal sentiments and decided against voicing her opinion on the topic of Frances' impending marriage. "It is unfortunate that she feels compelled to accept his offer because of the approaching Season's end."

"I should hope so after *two* Seasons—if she were to face another year . . . she would need to put herself on the shelf despite the difficulties it might cause for you to make a suitable match."

"Frances is hardly to blame, Auntie." Eugenia fully understood why her first Season had turned into her sister Frances' second. "Lord Aldolphus proved to be quite unworthy. He postponed the wedding until Frances had no choice but to hand him the mitten."

"If Frances had not behaved as if she were entitled to every luxury—I may be mistaken but she is not the Princess Royal. Although she may behave as if she were."

Eugenia could not disagree regarding the manner in which Frances conducted herself, always a bit high in the instep.

"I must admit that misguided pride runs in the family . . . and if it is not unreasonably high expectations then fanciful notions drift through the young girls' minds." Aunt Rose's gaze wandered to her grandniece, accompanied by a lifted eyebrow and a curt nod of her head.

Had that comment been directed at Eugenia? *Fanciful notions indeed!*

Aunt Rose's gaze rested on her clasped hands. "It was her last chance—she was in the right to accept— she had no option, really. Frances was lucky to have found Sir Russell. His income is not large but I'm sure they will manage quite well . . . in the end."

They sat quiet during the remainder of the journey. Eugenia grew sleepy with the lack of conversation. She never imagined that traveling could be so dull.

How her boredom would have been alleviated if only they were held up by a highwayman. Of course he would have been a very handsome one.

How exciting that would have been!

Eugenia was certain he would have abandoned his criminal ways right there and then at the sight of her. He would ignore their valuables and insist he have her heart instead.

How very romantic that would be.

She sighed at the very idea of the danger and excitement of their life together. Then she thought of how her parents would never approve of an outlaw as a suitable match for her. Nor would she be happy spending the remainder of her life avoiding the law.

Eugenia blinked, coming out of her reverie and gazed out the window. Perhaps it was best that she and Aunt Rose had an uneventful journey.

Many hours passed before the undisturbed, pastoral country landscape gave way to more frequent crossroads, occasional farms, and homes. Soon they observed small villages and ultimately signs of a great number of inhabitants populating the city of Brighton itself upon their arrival.

The carriage turned down a long drive and toward a modest brick cottage. Eugenia learned that her aunt had rented Grove House, a twelve-room residence complete with seven servants, for their stay.

"See here, Genie." Aunt Rose stood before the large window in the front parlor that displayed a splendid view of the Steyne. "I daresay our guests will enjoy this sight when they come to visit."

The concept of *their guests* sounded peculiar. Eugenia did not know a soul here in Brighton. She could not even imagine what kind of people would grace their interim home.

"We shall end our day with a small supper and retire early in preparation of a busy week to come."

Eugenia did not argue. To be honest, she was too tired to do much except sit with her aunt and share a small repast before heading off to bed.

"Is there anything else, my lady?" Katrina, Aunt

Rose's maid, followed Eugenia after supper and helped her settle into her room. "Your aunt, Mrs. Templeton, gave me instructions I was to see to your every comfort."

Exhausted from the day's travel and the anticipation that Brighton would provide more excitement than the isolated existence of Langford Hall, perhaps Eugenia had appeared as if she was in need of aid.

"I only thought . . . ," Eugenia began. "I don't know . . . I had hoped there would be something more awaiting us upon our arrival."

"Yes, indeed there will be. Mrs. Templeton has always preferred the evening entertainment here than in Town." Katrina nodded. "Guests from London come to Brighton to relax after the strenuous months of the Season."

Eugenia sat on the bed and listened.

"To be sure . . . there are private parties and assemblies," Katrina went on, sounding as if she had attended those activities herself. "There is a public tea, a promenade on Sunday, and card games several days during the week. The Castle Inn has a masquerade ball the first of every month, which I daresay is quite exciting!"

As fatigued as she felt, Eugenia thought that sounded wonderful and she could hardly wait.

"I am certain it shouldn't be too long before the

Master of Ceremonies will pay a visit to this very house and deliver a personal invitation."

Eugenia hoped so. She fell into bed but had trouble sleeping the first night. Overtired from traveling and anxious for her life in Brighton to begin, she finally drifted off to sleep, trying to imagine the glorious balls and the fabulous parties that would occupy the many days to come.

The next morning, Aunt Rose informed her niece of plans to attend a card party that evening. A card party? That was not at all what Eugenia had in mind.

"Auntie, why do we not go to the assembly?" Eugenia asked over her cup of chocolate. She was sure the Master of Ceremonies whom Katrina spoke of last night would call that very day.

"There is time, dear. There is time," Aunt Rose stated amicably.

"But there is a ball at the Castle Inn. Why do we not plan to attend?" Eugenia could not understand why they needed to wait.

"We shall go, my dear. We shall go—all in good time." Aunt Rose donned her hat and took up her reticule. "I'm off to the lending library. Do you wish to join me?"

"No, Auntie, you go on—and please enjoy yourself." Eugenia had no doubt her aunt had already paid her subscription dues far in advance.

The lending library? Eugenia sighed. She could not have imagined anything more dull.

Eugenia realized there was no avoiding the card party that evening. What she had expected to be a simple gathering turned out to be quite a crush with an astonishing number of people in attendance.

She partnered her aunt for a few hands. Eugenia normally enjoyed cards but this evening, with all the people, she was simply distracted beyond belief.

"This is quite enough. Here, now, come with me." Aunt Rose scolded her grandniece then ushered her from the card room to the refreshment room. "I did not attend to observe this dismal display of skill."

"I am sorry, Auntie." She felt her aunt's loss was entirely her fault. "I'm afraid I'm not very attentive this evening."

The real problem, Eugenia decided, although there were many who attended, was the lack of guests her own age. No sooner had that thought occurred to her when Aunt Rose led her to one side and made an introduction.

"Eugenia, dear, this is Lady Coddington and her daughter, Lady Penelope."

"I am very happy to make your acquaintance, Lady Eugenia." Lady Penelope glanced around them. "I'm afraid this gathering seems to be missing . . ."

Eugenia waited, curious to what opinion her new

acquaintance would voice regarding the guests attending card party.

"... youth." Lady Penelope took the liberty and linked her arm through Eugenia's. "Let's take a turn about the room, shall we?"

As she stepped alongside Lady Penelope, Eugenia noticed the two of them stood about the same height. Her new friend was very pretty. Lady Penelope's hair was perhaps a touch darker, her blue eyes sparkled, and her rosebud lips must have been the envy of all.

"I believe we have very many things in common," Lady Penelope began.

"We do?" Eugenia knew nothing of Lady Penelope.

"You are the daughter of the Earl of Langford, are you not?" Lady Penelope asked directly.

"Yes."

"I am the daughter of the Earl Coddington—we are both middle children, are we not?"

"I have an elder and younger sister," Eugenia declared. Perhaps they would not be well-known to one another, but it would be very nice to have at least someone known to her when she arrived in Town.

"My siblings are brothers, but I am nonetheless the middle child." Lady Penelope brightened as she announced, "I am to come out at the approaching Little Season."

"I'm to have my come-out during the Little Season

as well!" Eugenia grew more excited that she might have discovered a true friend.

"Your aunt is Mrs. Templeton?" Lady Penelope gazed at Eugenia's elderly relative who stood with her mother in deep discussion.

"She is my great-aunt, to be precise," Eugenia clarified. "My mother's aunt."

"Do you see that woman in the feathered turban looking at them?"

Eugenia regarded the lady taking extraordinary interest in her aunt and Lady Coddington.

"That is the Countess Tynsdale. She's concerned her position with my mother will be usurped by Mrs. Templeton." Lady Penelope giggled.

"Why ever should she worry about my aunt?"

Lady Penelope blinked at Eugenia. "Why they are currently the best of friends and Mrs. Templeton threatens that position. She is much better liked in society than the countess." Lady Penelope gestured again to their relatives. "See how there are so many people waiting to speak to her?"

"She does appear to be quite popular." A small crowd had gathered around the two ladies. Aunt Rose seemed to be more occupied with the guests than the cards.

"I suppose if one traveled as much as your great-aunt, one would meet anyone who is of any consequence sooner or later." Lady Penelope turned back to Eugenia. "I believe she met my mother in Bath ages ago. Her mother—my grandmother—introduced them."

Aunt Rose had never spoken of her connection with Lady Coddington nor did she, it occurred to Eugenia, speak of any persons in particular.

"It is a pity that our families were never close. You see, I believe that even the most casual acquaintances can be beneficial to one's position. From what I hear, your aunt is greatly admired. It is entirely possible she may know Prinny himself!"

Eugenia couldn't imagine anyone she knew would know the Prince Regent personally.

She and Lady Penelope reached the far corner of the refreshment table and turned to walk along the perimeter of the room, heading toward the card games.

"Perhaps we are destined to become fast friends!" Lady Penelope cried. "Here and now in this little town, we must acquaint ourselves with the eligible gentlemen. Once we two arrive in London for the Little Season, we shall reacquaint ourselves with them and both make perfect matches!"

Yes, that sounded quite splendid. Eugenia would love to have a close friend, especially in a place where she knew no one. She considered what Lady Penelope had said. Indeed, one could never truly know what might come from a casual meeting. Lady Penelope might make an advantageous marriage to a duke and then Eugenia would be the very good friend of a duchess!

The evening came to an unsatisfactory end when Aunt Rose halted their coze to announce to Eugenia, "I am ready to leave now, dear."

"Now?" Only minutes after making her first friend since arriving—perhaps her greatest friend.

"I am so very fatigued and there are so many arrangements to make for tomorrow."

Tomorrow? How could Eugenia think of tomorrow when tonight might have held so many possibilities?

First thing the next morning, Aunt Rose made sure the staff clearly understood there would be plenty of tea on hand. Then with her next breath she continued, "Cakes and sandwiches, and oh, yes, fruit tarts, ample fruit tarts. Strawberry, current, and apricot. Have Cook bake plenty. I shan't have my callers going away unsatisfied!"

"Do you really think we'll have many callers?" Eugenia naively asked. How was she ever to know what to expect? Did everyone who said they would stop by truly stop by?

Aunt Rose leveled one of her knowing looks at her niece. It made Eugenia feel as if she were seven years old again.

"They'll come," Aunt Rose said with a regal air. "They'll all come."

Promptly at 11 o'clock they had their first visitor. Each and every person they had met last night who said they would call was true to their word. Lady Penelope arrived with her mother Lady Coddington.

"I usually do not accompany my mother on her calls," Lady Penelope explained to Eugenia, "but I knew she planned to see your aunt and I wanted to meet with you again."

"I am so very glad you came. I'm afraid I do not find my aunt's acquaintances as entertaining as she—and they have been here for . . . hours it seems." But, of course, it couldn't have been.

"Well, they've all overstayed their welcome." Lady Penelope glanced about them before suggesting, "What do you think about you and I paying a visit to the lending library? I believe it is just down the street?"

"Is that not equally as tiresome?" Eugenia replied, totally exasperated at her new friend. "I cannot imagine anyplace more uninteresting!"

Lady Penelope persuaded her that they should leave. Eugenia did not put up much of a fight when pressed to collect her pelisse, hat, and reticule before accompanying her friend out the front door.

"My dear, Lady Eugenia." Lady Penelope grasped Eugenia's hand and pulled her near as they strolled down the front walk of the house. "I believe you are quite mistaken—you truly do not understand."

Eugenia had to admit that it felt good to step out of the house and move about after hours of sitting and entertaining visitors. The company of Lady Penelope made the short foot journey all the more enjoyable. Twenty minutes later they had arrived.

The lending library was not at all similar to the one Eugenia visited at home where one simply borrowed books. Here ladies and gentlemen not only found books but enjoyed tea and one another's company. Lady Penelope could not have been more correct.

There were so many people deep in conversation and Eugenia could easily imagine being one of them. Filled with worthwhile, pleasurable activity, she thought this was where she could spend many a pleasant afternoon.

Brighton seemed to be the perfect place to wait out the interval before attending the Little Season in the fall. Her stay here may even work to her benefit.

It might have proved impossible for Eugenia to appear anything but a country miss because her younger years were spent in the country. She often wondered if it would set her apart from the others, who seemed comfortable in a mixed social setting. Here in Brighton she might acquire a dusting of the much-needed town bronze.

Furthermore, it could be entirely possible to meet a suitable *parti* here in Brighton, as Lady Penelope had previously suggested. Eugenia would not dismiss the notion nor place a light emphasis on the chance occurrence *if* she were lucky enough to have it happen to her.

Chapter Two

The collection of calling cards that had accumulated that afternoon was not to be believed! Aunt Rose fanned out the invitations on the table for Eugenia to see on her return from the lending library.

There must have been at least a dozen to choose from. Eugenia tried to imagine what parties awaited her—balls, soirees, and routs! Perhaps she would attend a garden party, the theater, or perhaps give bathing in the ocean a try!

Before she left with her mother, Lady Penelope urged Eugenia to choose her evening diversions carefully—and, of course, they would wish to attend the same parties.

While perusing the invitations, Mr. Forth, the Master of Ceremonies called. He invited Aunt Rose and

Eugenia to the masquerade ball, occurring at the Old Ship Inn the Thursday night after this. The assembly room would be providing their guests with masks and dominos at the front door.

Just the mention of the approaching ball brought Eugenia to despair regarding her wardrobe. She could not help but feel that the gowns she had brought were so plain and would not do.

Although she lacked the skill to do her own alterations, she would instruct Aunt Rose's maid Katrina to drop the shoulders on her pale blue muslin and add a double-gold soutache to her dark green silk. That, Eugenia thought, should be sufficient.

"This evening we shall share dinner with my dear friends Mr. and Mrs. Penshurst before her musical fete," Aunt Rose told Eugenia, completely ignoring the remaining plateful of invitations.

Why on earth would they share dinner with an *old friend* when they had this plethora of invitations from which to choose? Surely there would be some more desirable entertainment to pass that evening.

Is that not what Aunt Rose had promised her? Surely she must have known just how much Eugenia wished to visit the ballrooms?

However, it did not signify. Not one complaint passed through Eugenia's lips as she dressed to accompany her aunt. She accepted her fate and consoled herself, knowing that she need not wear her best frock to this type of function, deciding that her dark green silk with the short puffed sleeves would suffice.

To her surprise Lady Penelope attended, which improved the prospects of the evening greatly. Eugenia believed that there would not be a dull moment if she were in the company of her friend.

At the musicale, they met the hostess' daughter, Miss Cynthia Penshurst. Eugenia found her to be quite companionable and was delighted to include Miss Cynthia in their little tête-à-tête.

Miss Cynthia told Eugenia and Lady Penelope that her elder sister had married last year. After the wedding, she and her parents left for the Continent, where they came across the musician Franz Mueller. Her mother was so completely transformed by his music and believed his talent was a gift to be shared!

And that was how he came to be in England.

"He's Austrian, very quaint, old-fashioned—and very talented. I believe he plays four or five instruments . . . perhaps more." Miss Cynthia glanced about as if some clue were to step forward. "The Prince Regent summoned him by *Royal* command our first week here."

"Really?" Lady Penelope leaned forward with growing interest. "The Prince, you say?"

"Please allow me to introduce him to you." Miss Cynthia motioned him to approach. A round-shouldered man in a powered wig neared. "Lady

Penelope, Lady Eugenia, may I introduce Herr Mueller."

Herr Mueller clicked his heels, and with a curt nod of his powdered-wigged head, acknowledged the two young ladies. "*Das* pleasure *ist* entirely mine."

It was immediately clear to Eugenia, by Lady Penelope's unpleasant expression, that her new friend had taken an immediate dislike to this man.

"Miss Cynthia tells us you recently played for the Prince Regent." Eugenia ignored her friend's reaction and hoped it passed Herr Mueller's notice.

"Ah, yes, at his Pavilion *von* evening. His Highness was so generous." Herr Mueller placed his hand upon his chest. "*Und* he did me the honor of accompanying me on his cello."

"Really?" This news awed Eugenia. "You must be a truly wonderful musician. Miss Cynthia here tells us that you are magnificent!"

Lady Penelope scoffed, glanced heavenward, and remained unimpressed.

"She *ist* too kind," he replied with a gentle smile. He was humble, almost bashful.

"He is being modest," Miss Cynthia returned. "Tell them how you performed throughout most of the Continent." She turned toward the ladies, anxious that they should know, and told them herself, "And he has played with many of the famous composers and for many of the Crown Heads of Europe."

"Please, Fräulein *Zin*-thia." His downcast gaze,

which had never reached their faces, adhered firmly to the floor. "You are being too kind."

"Mother insists he treat us with several selections on the harpsichord and violin this very evening," Miss Cynthia stated quite proudly. "Please, Herr Mueller, you must relay at least one of your stories to my friends."

"Your friends?" Herr Mueller glanced up at Lady Penelope, then at Eugenia, and decided to give in to Miss Cynthia's insistence. He relayed a tale of his travels.

One had to pay particular attention when conversing with the visitor. His thick German accent made him difficult to understand. It took a great deal of effort for the ones who listened.

Since Eugenia did not understand a single German word, with the exception of *Hessian,* she interrupted and reminded him to enunciate and slow his speech further. She did not wish to miss a single word of his interesting travels.

Herr Mueller was especially difficult to understand when he decided to pepper his anecdote with native words or phrases. Eugenia stopped him each time and had him translate for them.

While in the midst of his discourse, Herr Mueller gave Eugenia a most peculiar look.

"It is impolite for a . . . gentleman to stare at a lady," Miss Cynthia enlightened him.

Eugenia did feel a bit uncomfortable at his lingering

gaze but forgave him because she thought he might not know of their customs.

"*Verzeihung*, I do not mean to offend." He nibbled on the end of one of his fingers. "I think perhaps I have zeen you zomewhere before."

"I really do not think so," Eugenia said, certain that she would have remembered someone of his peculiar nature.

"You see, there." He pointed across the room. "*Und* my patroness beckons me now." He sharply bowed his head to each of them. "*Entschuldigung Sie, bitte*, you must excuse me. Until later." He clicked his heels again with a final curt nod and departed.

"Wasn't he an odd little man." Lady Penelope squinted in his direction. "Why does he wear that horrid wig? Doesn't he know it makes him look positively ancient?"

"He simply will not part with it." Miss Cynthia told them. "I think he believes it makes him appear more respectable. Perhaps the illusion of being one of the old masters."

"It does not signify. He's definitely a foreigner, without a doubt," Lady Penelope uttered in a snobby, entirely unpleasant tone. "And he is not handsome in the least. He is quite unexceptional."

"You are being most unfair and very unkind," Eugenia scolded her, keeping her voice soft.

"As a matter of fact," Lady Penelope stated even louder, "the shape of his face, his countenance, and bearing in general, reek of a commoner. What matter is it that he has kept company with royalty? He is nothing but a mushroom."

"Please, that is beyond rude!" Eugenia was beginning to feel that she had less in common with Lady Penelope than she'd thought. The sole aspect they shared was that they both were earls' daughters and that small matter was purely by accident of birth.

"He doesn't even have the decency to stand up straight in our presence! Can you imagine?" Lady Penelope continued. "The inelegant slouch!"

Herr Mueller did not have the statuesque posture of an English nobleman nor did he quite meet their eyes when he spoke. Eugenia thought him a bit shy, she would never think less of him because he was a foreigner.

With the way Miss Cynthia had gone on about his talent, Eugenia had looked forward to hearing Herr Mueller perform. Even before he sat to play, Aunt Rose alerted Eugenia that she wished to leave.

Eugenia was sure she did this on purpose.

Aunt Rose waits until I'm at the ultimate point of my enjoyment during the evening, then up and announces, "Eugenia, dearest, it's time we be off."

She found it most perplexing.

How had Aunt Rose gotten anywhere in Society when she did not stay through the evening?

It was just as well. Eugenia decided that if she sat through the musical performance, she might have caught some young man's interest. That might have proved problematic. After the musical performances he would search out the hostess and beg her for an introduction.

Eugenia had no doubt he would then court her, try to win her over, but she would not give him any indication of her affections. She would not wish to attach herself to anyone before attending the Little Season. Of course, she would bid him and this sleepy seaside city adieu then depart for London.

It should be quite tragic. She probably would never see the poor lad again.

If their paths should cross, she would be quite civil but not overfriendly. He may never be able to give his heart to another for the rest of his life. He might be the first of a long line of shattered hearts she would leave in her wake as she blazed a path into next Season.

It was just as well Eugenia left the card party early with Aunt Rose.

The next afternoon, Eugenia and Lady Penelope accompanied Miss Cynthia to the lending library. Miss Cynthia stepped away to return a book at the desk. Eugenia and Lady Penelope stood off to one side, trying to stand out of the way of the passing foot traffic.

Eugenia distinctly heard her name being uttered ever so softly. She glanced about but saw no one.

"Look there." Lady Penelope pointed into a tall bookcase. "Is that not Herr Mueller?"

To Eugenia's surprise, there he was peering between neatly stacked books on a shelf.

"*Und* Lady Penelope, it *ist mein* good fortune to see you also!"

Lady Penelope tried very hard to ignore the hail. She must have imagined that if she did not notice him, he might cease his torment. Concentrating on the shelves before her, she trailed her finger along the book spines, staring with increased intensity, showing that she had not heard him.

"Come now, Lady Penelope, we cannot be rude," Eugenia scolded.

"You may not be able to speak what you truly feel but I assure you I can." She took a few steps down to the next shelf and resumed her intensive search.

Eugenia watched a large book disappear from the shelf to the other side and a pair of eyes took its place.

"Lady Eugenia? *Das ist* you?" The brows arched and lowered as the speaker, in a heavily accented voice said, "How *wunderbar* to see you! *Bitte, warten Sie.*" The tome was quickly replaced and the staccato sound of footfalls told her of his impending approach.

This must have been where Herr Mueller had seen her previously. With the surrounding people and bookcases she must not have noticed him.

She resisted, complaining through the entire effort

as Eugenia pulled on Lady Penelope's reticule strings, returning her friend to her side.

"I do not want to—" Lady Penelope protested through clenched teeth.

"*Und* a good day to you as vell, Lady Penelope." He greeted her with a broad smile and a deep bow.

"Oh—good afternoon, Herr Mueller," Eugenia returned, trying to sound cheerful but in actuality she felt ashamed at her friend's behavior, and a bit nervous that Lady Penelope might say something hurtful.

"Whatever are you doing here?" Lady Penelope managed to sound civil.

"Same as you, *Fräulein.*" He sounded thrilled to have run into them. "Roaming *das* shelves for enlightenment. Hoping to meet friends who drop by *und* gossip."

"Gossip? Not I," Lady Penelope gasped.

To enjoy gossip is one thing. For others to know one enjoyed it was entirely another. Eugenia wished Herr Mueller had not said that to Lady Penelope. Miss Cynthia took this moment to join them, which was of great relief.

"*Guten Tag*, Herr Mueller," she said.

"Miss Zin-thia!" he proclaimed as if she were an undiscovered jewel. He gave a curt nod and clicked his heels, acknowledging her.

"Well, now that you have finished your business and have successfully found us, I believe it's time to be off," Lady Penelope said, giving Eugenia a gentle nudge.

"Must you? *Wirklich?* I vas hoping you would share tea vish a humble musician such as myself." He gave them the most forlorn expression.

Eugenia had only seen such a look on a dog denied a bone. Miss Cynthia gazed at Lady Penelope then Eugenia, pleading that they accept Herr Mueller's kind offer.

They were not in a hurry to leave nor did they have any pressing engagements. Eugenia sent a forlorn glance at Lady Penelope for some compassion. Would she not reconsider just this once?

Apparently Lady Penelope was quite adept at masking what she genuinely felt she as acquiesced. "Yes, of course. We'd be delighted," she lied.

Herr Mueller led the ladies to a table and took a seat with them. It seemed to please him to no end.

"Please, ve are all such gut friends, you must call me Franz."

"Yes, Franz!" Miss Cynthia echoed, very excited. "And you shall be Penelope and you, Eugenia!"

"I really do not think it proper, Herr Mueller," Lady Penelope lowered her voice and replied in all seriousness. "We, the ladies, perhaps might manage but . . . you are a . . . *gentleman.* I cannot see how it is in any way acceptable to polite Society."

He exhaled and appeared deflated at the news. "Perhaps you are correct. I apologize to you."

"Oh, Franz . . ." Cynthia empathized with him then offered to make him feel better. "Please, I insist all of you call me Cynthia."

"Well, he is known to you," Penelope pointed out. "But we have only *just* met him. I maintain that it cannot be proper for Eugenia nor I to be on such intimate terms."

"I understand." Franz managed to hold his chin high and accept Penelope's reasoning.

The ladies stayed for only half an hour before making their excuse that they needed to prepare for that night's ball. The masquerade ball Eugenia had so been looking forward to was to take place at the Old Ship.

The three young ladies planned to meet once inside. Franz, who, with a great deal of enthusiasm, could not wait to meet up with the ladies once again, told them he was invited to play at least once during the evening.

Eugenia and Cynthia cheered with great anticipation.

It was not beyond Penelope to feign delight at his expected presence.

Eugenia started her thorough and laborious toilette soon after arriving at Grove House. She was to attend a ball—a masquerade ball! It would be the night of her dreams! She would meet young men and dance until dawn.

Before entering the Old Ship's elegant ballroom, Eugenia donned a domino. She felt as if every eye focused upon her anonymous form. She found Cynthia and Penelope shortly after her arrival. No sooner did Eugenia greet her new friends than they were deluged with a dozen admirers.

"We cannot possibly dance with them all!" Cynthia appeared overwhelmed by the attention and could say nothing when a blond, curly-haired Romeo squired her away.

Eugenia had only dreamed of this kind of notice. Never did she imagine it would truly happen. A dashing, masked man bowed, took her hand, and escorted her to the dance floor.

"Speak for yourself, Genie," Penelope called to her while passing with a dance partner of her own.

They spent a good part of the masked portion of the ball amusing themselves with the young men. Eugenia could not say any of the gentlemen struck her as memorable—they all looked too similar. Nor could she swear that she did not dance with any of them more than once.

"I do not believe I can stand up for another set." Trying to catch her breath, Cynthia stood stock-still next to Eugenia. "Refuse them, Genie, refuse them all!"

Eugenia laughed at her friend's edict. The two masked gentlemen approaching the ladies halted when she waved them away, refusing their attention.

"Where is Penelope? Is she still dancing?" Cynthia glanced around and laid her hand on Eugenia's arm, steadying herself. "Or has she returned?"

"Somewhere, out there"—Eugenia gestured to the dance floor—"is Penelope among the dozens and dozens of prancing couples."

They stood quiet for a moment, watching the guests.

"Were any of the gentlemen you danced with noteworthy?" Cynthia's attention remained fixed on the guests stepping about in time to the music. Perhaps she was still searching for signs of Penelope.

"I must confess, without the benefit of seeing their entire faces, they seem much alike. Can you say any one gentleman has gained your favor?" As Eugenia waited for an answer, she felt Cynthia grip her arm more tightly.

Cynthia's eyes widened behind her mask and a strange look came across her friend's face. The odd thing of it all was, Cynthia wasn't looking at her. Her stare passed over Eugenia's shoulder and stretched far beyond where they stood.

Curbing her half-curious, half-terrified, completely overwhelming feeling on confronting the apparition, Eugenia turned slowly to see what had attracted Cynthia's attention. All of a sudden, she faced it . . . him.

She felt as if time drew to a standstill. There was a man. A tall, slender, dark-haired man with a stray lock curled upon his forehead. A man worthy enough to inhabit one of Eugenia's fantasies.

He made his approach, moving with such smoothness and grace across the room. His cape billowed around him and the mask obscured half his face. His mouth, in a dreamy half smile, greeted Eugenia.

The piercing, intense gaze from his dark eyes captured hers. Eugenia felt her neck warm and her cheeks flush. Incapable of movement, she did not think she could have fainted even if she had wanted to.

Once she'd laid eyes on this stranger, Eugenia had not drawn a single breath. Then, ever so slowly, movement from the people around them began.

His hand reached out for her. All this felt as if it were happening for a very long time, which proved most fortuitous. It gave her ample opportunity to put to memory the intricate engraving of his gold signet ring.

As soon as he took her hand, Eugenia felt as if her feet had left the ground. He took her into his arms and she felt as if they floated on air across the dance floor. The entire incident seemed very fuzzy, as if it were a dream. But she knew it all to be quite real.

After their dance, he placed a kiss upon her hand and uttered a polite thank-you. He turned from her, strode off the dance floor, and exited through the door from which he had come.

Just like that . . . he was gone.

Chapter Three

*W*ho *was that man*? Eugenia wished she knew!

Penelope rose Eugenia out of her surreal stupor to tell her it was time to remove their masks. Eugenia was anxious to do so and discover the identity of her stranger.

"Did you *see* him?" Eugenia anxiously asked Penelope. Penelope? Where had Cynthia gone?

"See him? How could one not see him?" Penelope replied in equal excitement. "Dearest Genie . . . he was so . . . so . . . ." But words failed her.

Although he seemed very real to them, when they made inquiries about him to the other ladies, they did not seem to recall seeing this mysterious dark-haired man.

That was impossible.

Eugenia was certain that if the other guests had seen him, they would certainly have remembered him.

She was grateful Penelope had seen him at the end of their dance. Cynthia, who was the first to see him, watched as he and Eugenia had stepped onto the floor. It reassured Eugenia that she was not going mad, had not brought him to life from her fertile imagination.

As she and Penelope walked back to the ball-room, Eugenia fanned herself. Just talking about the stranger caused her face and neck to warm.

"You must find him," Penelope told Eugenia. "If it is the sole accomplishment of the evening you must know who that man is. And I shall do all I can to help you."

With set determination, they strolled into the grand room together. On arrival, they noticed straightaway that no one was dancing. The guests stood silent, staring toward the musicians, the pianist in particular.

Cynthia sat next to her mother in the front row. At the pianoforte, Herr Mueller played a piece Eugenia had never heard with great flourish and in exquisite form. A small part of Eugenia regretted being tardy and missing the beginning of his performance.

"We are most fortunate, Genie," Penelope whispered to Eugenia. "We have an excellent opportunity to study all the gentlemen in attendance."

Indeed, all the guests stood or sat quietly, listening to the musical performance, making the task an easy one. Eugenia's gaze passed over the females standing among the gentlemen. She moved her attention from one gentleman's face to the next, looking for the familiar features she thought she remembered so well. He was nowhere to be seen.

Just as Franz put the finishing touches on the musical piece, Eugenia saw *him* standing in the far doorway that led into the card rooms.

"There he is!" Eugenia whispered and indicated the man across the room.

Penelope saw him immediately. He was leaning against the open door frame with a contemplative, gold-ring-adorned hand to his face.

"It *is* him." Penelope stared wide-eyed at him. Perhaps she thought he would disappear if she should blink.

"I wonder *who* he is?" Eugenia couldn't help but be curious. He looked to be someone of great consequence. If that were true, why would someone such as he single her out for a dance?

"I think you should find out," Penelope said with a tight smile. "That gentleman made quite a dramatic display to gain your attention. It is only fair that you should let him know he has done so."

Penelope's tone implied that what she really wanted to know was why Eugenia and not her? To tell the truth, Eugenia could not help but wonder that too.

He must have felt Eugenia stare at him. He returned her gaze along with an amused smile. Leaning toward his male companion, the stranger whispered to him.

Penelope dropped her fan open, hid the lower half of her face, leaned in, and whispered to Eugenia. "You need to lure him to you."

"What?" Eugenia fingered her fan, preparing to follow Penelope's instructions.

"Open your fan," Penelope repeated. "Draw it toward your face and gaze at him over the top."

Dropping her fan open, Eugenia glanced at her friend, checking to see if she was applying the fan correctly. She made the movements slow.

"Now tilt your head . . . and turn away from him ever so slightly."

Eugenia turned her shoulder and coyly dropped her gaze before abruptly returning her attention to his face. Even she knew that such obvious flirtations to one whom you have not been properly introduced would be considered scandalous.

"You need to let him know you are interested in making his acquaintance," Penelope urged.

Eugenia's actions seemed to have amused him. An absolutely sinful smile passed over his lips. Her message had been received.

"Well done!" Penelope praised Eugenia with a squeeze to her arm. "I believe you have successfully intrigued him. It looks as if he may be on his way here."

The music ended only seconds later. The guests milling about obstructed her view of him for the next several minutes. When the center of the room began to clear, Eugenia saw quite clearly that he moved in her direction.

She could feel a knot begin to tighten in her stomach. Eugenia wondered what had possessed her to take such daring action and tried to keep her wits about her.

Eugenia kept glancing at Penelope in a silent plea for help, but feared the kind of instruction she might receive. "Whatever am I going to do?"

"Why, Genie, you're going to introduce yourself." She smiled, seeming quite at ease.

Penelope left Eugenia gaping at the impropriety. She tried to catch her breath, still her heart, and settle her nerves before his arrival.

The throng of people thinned before her. Eugenia watched the two gentlemen continue their passage across the floor. The stranger's approach varied from his last.

During the first, Eugenia could see an almost predatory glint in his eye that entranced her by its sheer determination. This time, he merely strolled across the floor in a calm, casual approach.

He moved with the grace Eugenia vividly remembered. His arms swung by his side in perfect rhythm. His legs were long; he crossed the room in no time at all. His exuding self-confidence and refinement bespoke his breeding. She would not be surprised to learn that he was a gentleman of some consequence.

His intense stare should have frightened her. It was his dark gaze that first drew her attention, then her curiosity. Eugenia felt compelled to speak to him, with or without a proper introduction.

"Allow me to make myself known to you, ladies." Something about his voice sounded familiar . . . perhaps it was from what she could recall of the few words he had uttered to her on the dance floor.

Eugenia could not bring herself to look from him and glance toward the card room in search of the Master of Ceremonies or Aunt Rose to do the honors. How she had wished for a proper introduction.

"Thomas Mallick." The stranger sketched a bow. "Duke of Rothford."

Eugenia was suitably impressed, as was Penelope by her soft, sudden intake of breath.

"My friend"—he turned and gestured just so to imply the gentleman next to him—"The Honorable Donald Hamby."

Eugenia dipped a curtsy and introduced herself and Penelope in turn.

"So very pleased to make your acquaintance." Mr. Hamby bowed over Penelope's hand, then Eugenia's.

"May I suggest we remove to the refreshment room to remedy my parched throat?" Rothford suggested and he offered Eugenia his arm.

She hesitated but Penelope had already accepted

Mr. Hamby's escort and strolled past. Eugenia could not very well remain standing with the duke as their friends walked away. She took his arm and they followed.

The two couples found the refreshments and each partook of a glass of punch. Their conversation consisted strictly of socially acceptable, polite subjects and never neared a topic of a questionable or personal nature.

After a good half hour of pleasant conversation, the duke interrupted with sad news. "I am having such a delightful time, and I am quite distraught that I cannot stay to claim a dance. I am afraid Mr. Hamby and I must be off."

"Oh?" Was this some type of masquerade mystery game that they should deny they had shared a dance?

"Do you plan to attend the public tea on Sunday?" Rothford asked Eugenia.

"Well, we hadn't thought much about it," she answered.

Penelope leaned in. "I shall do all I can to persuade her that she must be present, Your Grace."

"Excellent!" Mr. Hamby remarked, quite happy with Penelope's answer.

Rothford then replied, "Perhaps we shall see you two lovely ladies there."

The gentlemen made their farewells and left.

"Of course he wants to meet you there," Penelope said with complete confidence.

Eugenia wasn't so certain. She thought he behaved exactly how a well-mannered man would, nothing more.

"A gentleman in his position cannot show partiality," Penelope stated. "He cannot *appear* anxious for your next meeting, even though he might have feelings to the contrary. I'm sure it must be as apparent to you as it is to me that he is more than overwhelmed at the thought of seeing you again." She showed more far more delight than the duke had. "It is so beyond . . . anything! He is a duke, Genie!"

"I am aware of that." Simply holding the position of duke did not secure her affection.

"How can you not be thrilled?"

"It's just that I find his reaction to me lacking." How Penelope could imagine that he showed any type of enthusiasm regarding Eugenia was beyond her.

"Do you not see that he must show some semblance of discretion?"

Was Eugenia to presume his less-than-stellar response was due to decorum and was only a pretense?

"You shall see," Penelope remarked with a nod. "We will just have to show some patience and wait to see how matters between the two of you progress."

We? Was not Eugenia the one, not Penelope, being pursued by His Grace?

Eugenia and Penelope were again beseeched to stand up with several gentlemen. They did the pretty.

As Penelope reminded Eugenia, "We can hardly disappoint them, can we?"

After the first dance set, Herr Mueller made his appearance in the ballroom. Eugenia was pleased to see him. Penelope made sure they did not cross paths.

"Is he not *très gauche?*" Penelope whispered confidentially to Eugenia. "It is one thing to share a few words with him at the library or to even sit next to him at a small dinner party, but to be seen at a large public assembly . . . We must think of our reputations."

Eugenia was less concerned about being seen with Franz and wondered how tarnished her reputation would be by keeping company with Penelope.

"He is so . . . out-of-date. At least one hundred years!" Penelope wrinkled her nose as if she had detected some unpleasant odor.

"I really do not think he is all that old." Eugenia suspected he was no more than five years her senior. She had to admit it was difficult to see the true nature of the man behind the brocade, powder, and rouge.

"That wig makes him look positively ancient! I cannot imagine how—"

As luck would have it, Aunt Rose took this most opportune time to interrupt. "It is time, Genie." Aunt Rose held out her hand for Eugenia.

This fortunate action spared Eugenia from being subjected to Penelope's never-ending list of the talented Austrian's failings on a personal level.

"Perhaps it is best you leave. You should thank your aunt for her early departure. I would." Penelope glanced at Cynthia and Franz who were heading in their direction. "It will save you from that horrid little man's uninteresting and endless discourse."

That night Eugenia had the most wonderful dream. She danced all night in Rothford's arms. Alone in the ballroom, on the deserted dance floor, the well-mannered duke abandoned the formal behavior he had displayed when they finally met.

She could feel the strength of his arm and the warmth of his hand on her back, holding her against him.

He wore the same mask. It hid the upper half of his face. Only the dark, sculpted curls atop his head and his lips were exposed. She reached up and stripped the mask away, only to find another in its place.

She all but exhausted herself making repeated attempts at unmasking him, only to fail. It felt heavenly to be in his arms, except she could not help but wonder who the real man behind the mask was.

Penelope insisted she and Eugenia visit Cynthia that very next afternoon to relay their discovery that the masked man at the masquerade was none other than the Duke of Rothford.

Cynthia had barely settled on the sofa cushion in

her family's turquoise and gold parlor before she asked, "Is he truly a duke, Genie?" Her wide-open eyes focused on Eugenia for an answer.

"You should have been there, Cynthia." Penelope gave the account of how the Duke of Rothford and his companion, the Honorable Donald Hamby, became known to them. It had been a critical gathering that Cynthia had missed. "The Duke saw to the introductions himself."

Cynthia gasped, covering her mouth in shock. "Say he didn't!"

"He did," Eugenia replied, not at all thrilled to make the confession. Penelope's version of her meeting with the Duke had more than a mere ring of gossip.

"And Genie shamelessly flirted with him," Penelope leaned forward to whisper.

"You didn't!" Cynthia drew in another quick breath and stared at Eugenia, shocked.

"She did!" Penelope appeared to enjoy adding her salacious enhancements wherever she could manage. "She used her fan with such skill."

"I was following your instructions!" Eugenia exclaimed in her defense. She was not the one who had the knowledge of such things.

"I did not hold a loaded pistol to your back," Penelope returned rather sharply. "I was only trying to help you do what you must."

Eugenia looked away. Perhaps she ought not to

have done it but that was beside the point. This was too cruel a reminder of her untoward behavior of the night before.

"But he did seek you out." Cynthia glanced to one side, apparently lost in deep consideration of Eugenia's circumstances. "And he made himself known to you, *without* a proper introduction and without the permission from your aunt. What if he should prove unsuitable?"

"Unsuitable?" The notion never occurred to Eugenia.

"Cynthia, he is a duke!" Penelope reminded her. As if one holding a title could not be loathsome and dishonorable in any way.

"There are those families who seek a wife's fortune to replenish their own. He would not be the first."

Eugenia blinked. "I have no fortune."

"But you do have a dowry," Penelope pointed out. "How much would Lord Langford's daughter bring?"

"*He* may not know. Then again, he may not care." Cynthia maintained her dubious air. "Perhaps he is overwhelmed by your beauty."

"You have enchanted him." Penelope stood and strolled to the window. "We may arrive together for the Little Season but you will be the fiancée of a duke."

And Aunt Rose thought Eugenia was the one who wove fanciful tales.

"The Little Season will begin with the grand

celebration of your forthcoming nuptials," Penelope elaborated. "Shall we be invited to the wedding?"

"I should hope so. We were with Genie when she and the duke first met." Cynthia grasped Eugenia's hand. "Will the banns be read that first Sunday or shall you be wed with a special license?"

"I cannot imagine he should want to wait longer than he needs," Penelope stated in complete confidence.

"I had wished for a wedding at St. George's." Eugenia's confession was a closely held secret. She had heard of well-known aristocrats marrying there and only dared dream that she could do the same.

"Oh, that would be grand." Penelope's faraway dreamy visage matched that of Cynthia's expression.

Eugenia hoped she had not succumbed to the same.

"And what of your gown?" Cynthia's voice took on the same dreamy quality of her face. "I had always wished for pale pink cotton with fine embroidery."

"I should have a silver satin dress, I think," Penelope mused.

"I have always dreamed of white silk and a bit of lace." Eugenia divulged another secret desire. "And flowers. Dozens, hundreds perhaps. Enough to fill the entire room!"

"Oh, yes, many, many flowers!" Cynthia cheered.

"Hothouse flowers," Penelope amended.

"Gardenias? Violets?" Cynthia supplied.

"Peonies," Eugenia continued. "And after the ceremony there would be a huge, wonderful, sumptuous breakfast."

"*Und* you should have music so *wunderbar* to express your love!" Herr Mueller then shuffled into the room, joining the ladies.

All three girls gasped and faced the door at the sudden male presence.

"Franz!" Cynthia squealed at the same time Eugenia cried out, "Herr Mueller!"

"Music?" Penelope intoned distastefully. Perhaps the distasteful part was meant for Herr Mueller himself and not his suggestion. "One does *not* have music at a wedding."

"Not usually, however, *das* may be in an arranged marriage. But Lady Eugenia and her duke such as this, when there is a meeting of two souls, it is not just a ceremony, it is a celebration of the heart!"

Eugenia sensed the truth in what Franz said.

"*Bitte*, tell me of your duke." He directed his question at Eugenia. "Do you find him charming? Handsome? Something more, perhaps?"

"He is charming," Cynthia affirmed, answering for Eugenia. "And most handsome."

"*Und* he *ist* a duke, therefore his position must be very desired among the ladies, no?"

"Of course he is desired!" Penelope's frustration

was accompanied by the scuff of the toe of her shoe against the carpet. "He is everything a girl should want."

"My admiration for Rothford does not come from his being a duke, it is . . ." Eugenia did not know exactly how to phrase her regard for him. "I must confess his appeal has nothing to do with his position or his physical appearance . . . There is something about him . . . I'm not sure I can say."

Franz leaned toward her as Cynthia and Penelope had, the trio hanging on her every word.

"There was something about the way he held me in his arms, the way he gazed into my eyes. It was very *personal.*" Eugenia could not explain what she had experienced in any other terms.

"You felt a connection . . ." Franz held his index finger in the air, making his point. "The meeting of two souls!"

"Yes, that's right." Eugenia could almost believe that was exactly what had happened.

Cynthia and Penelope sat mute, astonished at the dialogue between Eugenia and Franz. Whether the two friends did not know what to say, what to add to the conversation, or simply could not comprehend that Eugenia and Franz had reached such a level of mutual understanding left them as the onlookers.

"You see." Franz nodded, across his face passed a very peculiar expression Eugenia could not quite

identify. Then something appeared . . . a smile, perhaps? "Ahh," he intoned thoughtfully and motioned
his hands as if conducting an orchestra. "*Und* now
the composition of the duet begins."

Chapter Four

The next afternoon, Eugenia and Cynthia, sans Penelope, chose to frequent the lending library. As they entered, they stopped briefly to exchange pleasantries with several small circles of people sharing a quiet coze. They then ordered tea and found themselves an unoccupied table. No sooner did the tea arrive than Herr Mueller entered.

Summons from surrounding tables beckoned for the talented musician to join their group without success. Eugenia was quite sure the thought of sitting with someone else had never crossed his mind. How delightful for him that others should value his company, unlike Lady Penelope Coddington who could not have cared less if she ever set eyes on him again.

As the three of them sat enjoying their tea, Franz

rambled on while Eugenia daydreamed. She stared off toward the entrance and noticed the Duke of Rothford enter with two gentlemen. One she recognized as Donald Hamby and she heard them refer to the other as Foster.

Needless to say, Eugenia's disposition improved immensely upon seeing Rothford. Franz must have noticed too. He halted in midsentence to turn and see what or who had so completely captivated her attention.

"It's him," Cynthia softly announced. "Your gentleman from last evening. He—"

"Yes, it is the Duke of Rothford." Eugenia thought she could remain calm and unaffected by his presence but her heart raced as he neared.

The handsome trio headed in their direction and did not stop to greet anyone on their way to the back of the establishment. Eugenia had expected his manner would change the moment he saw her.

She was wrong.

Rothford did not acknowledge any of them.

Eugenia had thought his attention did not matter but the unbidden tears that welled up in her eyes as he passed her in silence told another story. She fumbled at her reticule for a lace handkerchief and blotted away her tears. It was so unladylike to cry in public.

She had expected some type of recognition from him.

"Oh, Eugenia, I am so sorry," Cynthia said soothingly. She set her cup down and laid a comforting hand upon her friend's arm.

"*Ist* this your duke?" Franz's eyes narrowed and his glare followed the men with interest.

"*My* duke, indeed!" Eugenia pouted, wiping the last bit of moisture from her eyes. She sniffed and lifted her chin in new found composure.

"I cannot believe he said nothing to you," Cynthia remarked quietly in disbelief.

"*Männer* from my country *vood* not treat a lady so." Franz's voice had a hard edge to it. He snatched the napkin from his lap and dropped it on the table. "*Verzeihung*," he said, shooting to his feet.

"Herr Mueller, please sit down!" Eugenia said, she hoped not too loudly. She did not wish to make her situation worse than it already was.

He understood the warning. His gaze met hers and he lowered himself into his seat at her silent request.

"Has he not disgraced you, *Fräulein*?"

"No, not at all," she responded curtly but felt the shame of being socially cut. "We have only shared a single dance together. I suppose I have construed something more." Eugenia rested back in her chair and felt quite ashamed.

He took to his feet again. "I vill not allow his insufferable action to pass. *Und* I insist you allow me to speak to him on your behalf!"

"No, please, Herr Mueller. I do not want you to

cause a scene!" She grasped his hand and, with a gentle tug, returned him to his seat. "I thank you for your gallant gesture."

Franz straightened his waistcoat and, once again, settled in his chair. "If you ever vish me to intervene, I shall be more than happy to oblige, *Fräulein.*"

It was then Eugenia realized she had under-estimated Herr Mueller and Penelope had completely misjudged him. It was there and then that Eugenia decided she should spend more time with the musician and not waste another thought on that dastardly duke.

That evening there was a rout at Countess Helms-ley's. Eugenia felt a certain trepidation in attending a function that might lure the Duke of Rothford. Still, she believed she could enjoy herself even in the event he should be present.

She could ignore him just as effectively as he had ignored her.

As she dressed for the evening, Eugenia had not made the effort for a thorough toilette. She dressed in her azure blue gown but had not made much of an effort with her hair. She pulled curly wisps around her face, allowing the dramatic contrast of her rich, dark hair against the smoothness of her flawless skin, and decided that it would have to do. She simply did not care how she looked tonight.

Aunt Rose wandered into Eugenia's room to check on her progress. "I have the most delicious necklace that would go splendidly with that gown," she tittered.

With that, Aunt Rose stepped out of the room and returned not more than three minutes later with an exquisite black velvet box. She pulled up on the lid and the heavy brass hinges groaned. The box opened to reveal a massive citrine sparkle. Lying on a pillow of pristine white satin were a necklace, bracelet, and ear bobs.

She removed the necklace from its resting place and laid it gently around her niece's neck. Eugenia gazed upon her reflection, noting that even the jewelry did not brighten her spirits.

"You shall do it justice, I think." Aunt Rose ran her hand over Eugenia's head, smoothing her hair in place.

After adorning Eugenia with matching bracelet, she announced, "You look splendid! Like a duchess!"

That was the last thing Eugenia wanted to hear.

"There, there, my dear, you will return to your usual lively self once you've danced a few sets," Aunt Rose assured her. "Next to jewelry, the attention of young men always makes you feel better!"

Eugenia did not wish to dance. She did not wish to hear music. She really did not wish to attend the party. However, Aunt Rose insisted.

Once they arrived, Cynthia did her best to cheer Eugenia, but to no avail. The several dances Eugenia managed did little to improve her disposition. It was only with Herr Mueller's constant attention and generous care that she began to feel a bit better.

Franz was perhaps not the most attractive of men. Most women might overlook his compassion and forbearance, which well compensated for his physical inadequacy. He did not seem threatening in a suitor type of way and perhaps that is why Eugenia found him so companionable.

Resting in a brocade chair, Eugenia sat away from the main festivities. Franz came and left with various distractions that might tempt her out of her current bout of the sulks. She sat quietly, her legs crossed at the ankles in a semislouched position. It was hardly ladylike.

She rotated the bracelet around her wrist, pushing gold-set stone after gold-set stone, admiring the small flashes of the yellow citrine reflecting in the dim light. Eugenia found the sparkles so distracting, she didn't hear the sounds of footsteps approach.

She startled as a pair of legs in cream-colored breeches appeared before her.

"I beg your pardon, Lady Eugenia. I did not mean to startle you."

It was the Duke of Rothford. And Eugenia had made a point of avoiding him.

"I do not think I ever gave you permission to address me, sir. We have not been properly introduced." She straightened in her chair.

Rothford reached for her arm and helped her stand.

Eugenia did not feel alarmed. She knew he wouldn't dare do anything threatening.

There was a roomful of people only a few feet away, well within calling distance. Not to mention, dear little Franz might return at any moment and come to her aid without even asking.

The Duke fingered the bracelet. "That's quite lovely, but it pales in comparison to your beauty." He then tucked her gloved hand in the crook of his arm and secured its placement, resting his hand over hers.

Across his face he wore a smile with an uncertain message, reminiscent of the first time she saw him, masked, crossing the room in her direction.

"I thought you might care to dance?" He already led her to the dance floor. His manner was too confident and very self-assured.

Eugenia wasn't sure she cared for it. "It might be nice if you had asked first, *sir.*" She had not yet graced him with a smile.

"I should like it very much if you called me Roth-ford," he drawled.

"I see no need to force familiarity when we are all but strangers, Your Grace." Eugenia tilted her chin into the air, showing him that she could be just as disagreeable with him as he had been to her.

"Do you really think so?" His tone was playful as if teasing her.

The strings struck up the beginning measures of a

waltz. Rothford wrapped his arm around her waist and gently pulled her close.

Eugenia wondered why he had acted so distant toward her earlier, yet he offered her no explanation. What purpose did it serve to encourage her one moment then turn his back and ignore her as he had that very afternoon?

After their dance, they removed to the terrace, still well in sight of the other guests. Rothford behaved quite gentlemanly while in her company.

"He was a business associate." The Duke finally offered to explain his earlier behavior at the library. And Eugenia thought his excuse had come a bit too late.

"It was quite important. I could not allow myself to become distracted." He applied a soft kiss to the back of her gloved hand. "I have no doubt that you would most certainly be a considerable distraction to me."

His eyes glistened while he charmed her. Eugenia knew exactly what he was attempting to do, and she did her best to fight its affects, but he was succeeding.

"If you would allow me to accompany you on the promenade tomorrow afternoon, I give you my word that I shall be entirely at your disposal."

Eugenia wanted to refuse but could not bring herself to deny him. "Very well." She turned away to prevent him from seeing her eyes growing moist. Was she happy he wanted to reacquaint himself with her?

Or was she relieved that she might mean something more to him?

"That's my girl." He bent over her hand and kissed it again.

It remained to be seen if she was *his girl* or not.

"Now I regret that I must depart. Only duty of a most serious nature could compel me to leave your side."

Leave? But he had only arrived. Eugenia wondered why, with his constant comings and goings, he bothered to attend these functions.

"I did not wish to part when there was unpleasantness between us." He gave a slight squeeze to her hand and whispered, "And I'm sure we have much more to look forward to in the days ahead."

Then he left her. Eugenia watched him walk away.

She fully planned to speak to Aunt Rose about him. Her dear beloved great-aunt, Eugenia had learned during their time together in Brighton, was not the odd, eccentric, antiquated woman she had once believed.

In reality, Eugenia had come to learn, not much escaped her shrewd relative. Wise beyond her three and sixty years, she socialized in only the most elite circles and took pride in her refined manner and exquisite good taste.

Although she may not have followed the rules of propriety—she did tend to have her own standards—she insisted others tread a straight and narrow path.

Yes, indeed. Her insight regarding the Duke of Rothford would be most appreciated.

The next morning at breakfast, Aunt Rose set her plate on the table, took up her coffee cup, and remarked, "If I am not mistaken, I believe you met with someone of consequence last night. Do not think that has passed my notice."

"I did not think it had." Eugenia sipped her chocolate and reminded herself that not much escaped her aunt. "I am acquainted with the Duke of Rothford."

"You might have made him known to me. It was not well done of you at all. He should have had your introduction through me. What type of a gentleman dispenses with protocol?"

"I'm afraid that the masquerade portion of the assembly had emboldened him." Eugenia was not about to relay the entire truth to her aunt. "He approached me for a dance."

Aunt Rose seemed to show a bit of interest. Did she not truly know how Eugenia and the duke had met? And here she thought her dear relative knew everything.

"Tell me true, Auntie, is that not the precise intent of a 'masked ball'? For the guest to make the acquaintance of those whom one would not, under ordinary circumstances, single out for attention?"

With his position, his interest in any woman would have been welcome. To admit Eugenia had with the help of Penelope, gone a step further to discover his identity, and how she had openly flirted with him, again aided by Penelope, would be quite beyond the pale.

"What concerns me is that His Grace has taken a great deal of interest in you. The Duke has already made several inquiries into your family and background." Aunt Rose did not look up from her plate when she spoke. "I cannot help but wonder if he is one of those peers with title and his pockets to let."

"A fortune hunter!" Eugenia's cup nearly slipped from her fingers. She was quick to believe that the truth. It would explain his occasional tepid behavior toward her. He only paid attention to her when it was advantageous to him.

The rogue! He did not care for her in the least!

"You may not be aware of this, my dear, but your dowry could settle the largest of debts and save a single dukedom with no difficulty," Aunt Rose remarked, quite unaffected that a rascal such as he was after her grandniece.

"I have made my own inquiries about this fellow," she continued. "I can assure you that he is more than financially well-off and possesses several estates. His country seat is in Kent and he resides there several months out of the year. He spends most of his time at his townhouse in Hanover Square, London. It seems he is very eligible and much sought after. Unlike many men of his ilk, his name is not besmirched by women or gaming."

Did he think he was better than other men? That Eugenia should feel fortunate he chose her to address?

"Now that we have found the Duke's status and reputation are beyond reproach, we must accept that any affection he may declare for you is genuine." Aunt Rose's smile rejuvenated her ten years. "And now that you know where his interests lie, I can just imagine how you would very much allow yourself to return his adoration."

Eugenia was not quite sure that was exactly what she had in mind. However it gave her a great deal to think about.

Mrs. Penshurst and Herr Mueller came to Grove House for tea that afternoon. When the elderly ladies' conversation became tedious, to Eugenia's great surprise, Franz exhibited unexpected perception by asking her to accompany him for a turn about the rear gardens. That removed them both from the elderly ladies' languorous company.

She was only too glad to escape. What a sweet man Franz was. Eugenia could not have been more thankful for his companionship.

"This *ist* quite splendid." He clasped his hands behind his back and took in the scenery. "I spend so much time inside practicing *und* performing . . . I am grateful for every opportunity to step outside *und* breathe the fresh air."

"I find it a pleasant way to occupy oneself."

"You saw your duke last evening, if I am not mistaken?" Franz mentioned casually. "*Und* most friendly. Then again, he *ist* your duke?"

"Rothford explained that he was busy with business affairs. It was just a misunderstanding." Eugenia feared Franz did not think too well of him since that day at the library when Rothford ignored her.

"I see." Franz nodded, contemplating her words. "*Und* you find this . . . Rothford's explanation to be acceptable?"

"Yes, I do." She took his placid smile to mean he was pleased regarding the outcome.

"*Gut.* Then I shall forgive him as well." He glanced about the surrounding skies, taking a closer look. "The air *ist* perhaps not as fresh as Austria. Alas I shall not complain, this *ist* out-of-doors." A few more steps and he said, "You must come to *mein* country one day. You vill like it very much. Until that time ve make preparations *und* first teach you the language. We begin vith a few words of German."

Eugenia laughed. "I don't think I can learn German. I am much more adept at French."

"Come now, *Fräulein*," he urged her. "You must try."

Eugenia learned that *bitte* means "please" and *danke schön* means "thank you."

"You see. It vill be no time at all before you can scold your lady's maid for burning your hair with the curling irons and reprimand your seamstress because your gown does not lay just so." He motioned to the length of his lower limb, illustrating where the offending imaginary garment rested.

"After I don my dress and have my hair curled, I suppose I should be expected to attend a ball?"

"Of course, *Liebling*." He chuckled, perhaps thinking he had convinced her that she should continue learning German.

Eugenia stopped short and stared at him. "*Liebling* . . . what does that mean?"

"It *ist* only an endearment." He glanced up at her through dark, white-powder-coated lashes as if he had taken a liberty. "If you rather I did not—"

"No, I find it acceptable." Eugenia glanced around them, making sure they were indeed alone, and bestowed upon him a shy smile. "When no one is near, if you please."

He reacted to the great honor with a wide grin, beaming across his face.

"Where were we?" Eugenia once again stepped forward, continuing their walk.

"Ah, yes, you ver acting like a churlish child, scolding your servants."

"I'll have you know that's ridiculous!" She sent him a playful, nasty glare through narrowed eyes then laughed at the absurdity. "You want to teach me the only phrase I should ever really need to know."

"And what should that be?" He focused his complete attention on her.

"I must know the phrase: 'May I have this dance?' or how ever shall I know when a gentleman is asking me to step onto the floor with him?"

Eugenia really hadn't expected that she should ever need it here or in London, but they were only playacting.

"Ah, yes, most ingenious." He stopped and faced her so she might watch the words form upon his lips. *"Darf ich Sie um diesen Tanz, bitten?"*

Franz repeated the words slowly—over and over, until Eugenia could easily say them.

"Now when I meet an extremely rich Bavarian Baron in London who can manage but only a few words of English . . ." Eugenia began the fanciful tale.

"He finds you . . . *die Schönheit* . . . so enchanting, he cannot keep himself from approaching you for a waltz," Franz continued on with the story.

"Then out of his mouth would come, *"Darf ich Sie um diesen Tanz, bitten?"* Eugenia repeated flawlessly. "Because you spent time teaching me bits of German, I will know exactly what it means! Then I will take his arm, curtsy"—Eugenia took

Franz's proffered arm and curtsied—"and reply, *danke schön.*"

"Then you vill dance." He partnered her for a few steps of the waltz.

Eugenia found it a slight bit awkward because they were roughly the same height. Normally gentlemen were a few inches taller and not looking directly into her eyes.

"From that single dance with the Baron there will be gossip." Eugenia stepped away from Franz. "The *ton* would want to know how I was able to speak to this foreigner."

"I do not see how such a thing can be avoided." Franz shrugged, falling into step beside her. "You *und* the Baron will be *on-dit* for weeks on end."

Eugenia squealed with laugher! Never had she heard, never thought of anything so absurd.

"The Baron might become quite popular after you dance vith him," Franz went on, not bothered by her outburst. "The matchmakers vill seek him out for their own daughters. In the end, dancing vith him vill be *wunderbar* for his reputation."

They giggled and laughed together. The entire scenario was outrageous.

"Franz, you are horrible for encouraging me," Eugenia scolded him.

Perhaps the episode of the Bavarian Baron would not occur, for Eugenia had already met the duke of her dreams here in Brighton. Although she doubted

Rothford would begrudge her one dance with a lonely foreigner, especially one of such noble birth. Eugenia knew that in the end she must break his Bavarian heart.

C'est la vie. C'est l'amour!

Chapter Five

Sunday was the Promenade at the Old Ship. Not only had Rothford kept his word but his lavish attention made Eugenia quite the envy of the whole affair.

"You are absolutely a sight to behold!" Rothford praised Eugenia's choice of a light blue sprig muslin then turned his attention to her hat. "And where did you get that delightful bonnet?"

"I purchased it yesterday right here in Brighton at Madame Marchaine's." Eugenia turned her head to give him an unobstructed view of her elegant headwear.

"Very nice. Very nice, indeed." He pulled her gloved hand through the crook of his arm and placed his hand over hers.

It did not bother Eugenia that he gently trapped

her hand in what could be construed as a possessive way.

"Will you object if I keep you all to myself?"

"Just for today, mind." Eugenia could not help but smile. It delighted her that he should say such a thing when she had begun to believe that he did not care for her.

They strolled along together. Eugenia felt right at home, dangling upon his arm as if he were a custom-made accessory meant for her. She could not have the slightest complaint regarding his behavior.

Occasionally he leaned close and whispered into her ear. Nothing of importance, just a little comment or observation that a man in his position might find amusing. Their familiar behavior might have shocked some people, although she did not notice any of the guests fall upon the floor in an apoplectic fit.

The farther they strolled and the more she thought about it, Eugenia grew to believe the Duke of Rothford was the man she had dreamed of all her life. Granted, he had not yet spoken of his love for her, but he must have felt the same as she.

And he had not kissed her as of yet.

To be honest, the duke had not even tried. And Eugenia had already decided she would allow him to kiss her. Why should she not? They were all but engaged!

Just as certain as she was regarding his affection, Eugenia knew Rothford would want to speak to her parents as soon as all parties involved had arrived in

London for the Little Season. Even though their initial introduction had not been a proper one, there were conventions to follow when it came to an engagement, and it all had to be done correctly.

The Duke would have his word with Papa. Then after receiving overwhelming family approval, Rothford would choose the most romantic spot in all of London to ask Eugenia the one important question: "Will you do me the honor of becoming my duchess?"

Rothford would be quite insistent, professing his love for her. He might try to bribe her with a trinket or two. Of course, in the end, Eugenia would say yes. She and the Duke would have the grandest nuptials of the Season!

"Lady Eugenia?" Rothford repeated.

"I'm sorry, my thoughts were drifting." She blinked and smiled up at him.

He gazed down upon her and said, "You looked as if you were a hundred miles away."

"Perhaps, but we were together, I can assure you." She giggled, thinking how silly her daydreams were but hoping they would come true all the same.

"That is comforting to hear." Rothford stopped and gestured to a nearby bench shaded by a tree where they should sit. "I'm afraid I have some sad news. I am again called to leave and we must part."

The news devastated Eugenia. She did not wish them to part just when his attentions were beginning to strengthen, just when she knew he was strongly attached to her.

"I am to leave in a few hours' time and I shall return in only a matter of days. I promise you shall scarcely notice my absence."

He might as well have said he planned to be absent for an eternity and travel to the ends of the earth!

"I suggest we do our best to put that unpleasantness aside and concentrate on enjoying this splendid outing together. I remain completely at your disposal."

Eugenia pretended his absence would not bother her in the least. She remained silent as he led her toward their friends Penelope and the Honorable Donald Hamby. The foursome shared a table, enjoying their tea.

Even though she could not staunch her misery at the Duke's impending departure, Eugenia knew she was the envy of every girl within sight. She could read it on their faces, sense it in their posture as their glances hardened.

After the tea, card games erupted in the adjacent room. She and Rothford sat for several hands. He was correct about enjoying each other's company for they passed the time in a pleasant manner.

Then she noticed his posture stiffen. His gaze darted past her and toward the doorway. She managed a sideward glance and recognized the man he had called Foster from the library. He stood at the door in a most awkward fashion as if he were trying very hard not to be seen.

Rothford folded his cards and laid them aside. A look and a nod from him told Eugenia to do the same. She did. The Duke made their apologies to the remaining players then led her outside to the garden.

They stepped under a white latticed gazebo. "It is time, my dear, for me to depart."

Eugenia decided that if he were to leave now, she would at least have some assurance of his affection. She wanted him to kiss her and spent her energies on looking as fetching and irresistible as she could manage. She tilted her head and gazed at him in pure adoration.

Rothford spoke to her, saying something of the particulars of his journey. All Eugenia cared about was that he would be leaving her again.

She pursed her lips into an adorable moue and batted her lashes to no avail. With only a kiss to the back of her hand and a fond adieu, he was off.

How *very* lowering.

A massive cloud floated overhead, blocking a great deal of the sun. The dimming light grew evident with every passing minute. Dismayed at her lack of appeal, Eugenia remained alone in the growing darkness.

Why would he leave her without expressing what he truly felt? What Eugenia *knew* he must feel.

Sigh after heartfelt sigh, she remained for some

number of minutes. Eugenia was not certain how long before she heard footfalls heading in her direction.

To her utter amazement, she instantly recognized the confident swagger and the familiar rhythmic swing of the arms. It was Rothford. He had returned.

She did not want to appear anxious at his reappearance and took great effort to restrain herself. Eugenia took a deep breath and held it. Slowly, she allowed it to escape and finally glanced casually up at him.

The filtered sunlight illuminated the garden. The lattice threw harlequin shadows across his face, giving him a dramatic cast. She was not sure what to expect from him and remained silent. Eugenia gazed up at him, giving him a chance to speak first.

"I wasn't entirely satisfied with our farewell," he said. His words were slow, almost impossible for him to utter. "Before I leave for . . ."

She stared wide into his dark eyes. "Amberly," she finished for him, anxious to see what direction he would take.

"Yes, Amberly," he echoed, staring deep into her eyes.

Every lucid thought in her head left. He sat very close to her on the bench. His proximity fended off the coolness of the deep shade of the cloud.

At that moment Eugenia felt as if they were of one mind, one heart.

"I shall miss you while I am away." His gaze ran over her face, caressed her shoulders, before returning to her eyes. "I shall only be gone for . . ."

"Three or four days at the most," again she answered for him. She was a mindless creature, finishing each sentence he began.

It was almost as if he had forgotten himself. Perhaps Eugenia had succeeded in distracting him as he had once accused her.

"It is only for a short while—no longer than is necessary, I can assure you," he whispered ever so softly. The volume of his voice grew only as he neared, for she felt his breath upon her ear with every word he spoke. "Then, with your permission, I shall take leave of you after a kiss."

Her eyelids became heavy and lowered. Her lips pursed ever so slightly in great anticipation of the long-awaited event. She felt quite the half-wit when he placed a chaste kiss upon her cheek.

He backed away but the retreat lasted only for a moment. Eugenia discovered the same disappointment that dwelled within her was mirrored in his dark, dreamy eyes.

With a sudden spark, she noticed a new determination overtake him. His hand slid to the back of her head, pulling her toward him until their lips met.

Disentangling her arms that somehow were wrapped around his neck, he pushed her away. The indiscretion left them both breathless. Eugenia knew it was not merely her reaction. She could hear him gasping for air, see the rapid rise and fall of his chest.

"I never should have allowed that to happen," he said, standing from the bench and stepping away.

Eugenia wasn't sure if he was speaking to her or to himself. She certainly did not regret their kiss.

"Please forgive me. I will not force my affection upon you again." He turned away then as if a second thought had occurred to him. He said, "Nor will I ever mention my atrocious behavior *ever.*"

Before she had a chance to protest, he left.

All Eugenia could think of was how wonderful it felt to lose herself in his arms, how wonderful it felt to kiss him—finally—after imagining it for so long. And how wonderful the next time would be. She promised herself there most certainly would be a next time.

In the days after Rothford's departure, Eugenia came down with a serious case of the blue devils. She managed with her day-to-day activities such as accompanying Cynthia to their usual rounds of shopping and the lending library. Eugenia found all their public outings completely tedious. She even found it possible to tolerate Penelope's capricious company.

Occasionally Herr Mueller included Eugenia on his daily constitutional. She imagined he must have nothing to occupy his time. Perhaps he was taking pity on her in her current state and wished to do his duty as her friend to make her feel better.

I must be horrid company.

Eugenia felt so out of sorts she even borrowed some books from the library and read them. She was not sure if this change was due to Cynthia's influence or from sheer boredom.

Franz continued to tutor Eugenia on her German. She could barely concentrate, her mind wasn't at all present, and she found it difficult to keep track of the days that passed.

The musician had been most amiable company and oftentimes she thought of him as a fixture and constantly underfoot. Then it seemed there were days when she hadn't seen Franz at all.

He did not confide in her of his schedule or where he kept himself, nor did Eugenia ask. She supposed he might have been practicing or perhaps Cynthia or Mrs. Penshurst monopolized his time. After all, being his benefactress, Mrs. Penshurst had every right.

Eugenia filled her empty hours with constant thoughts of Rothford. How his eyes sparkled when he gazed upon her and the timbre of his voice during their last meeting. She pictured the glint of his signet ring before she'd felt the warm touch of his hand brush against her cheek. She remembered the look on his face when his lips claimed hers.

She so looked forward to his return. The anticipation of his embrace was beyond words. If he did not curb his ardor, they would most certainly be forced to apply for a special license before the start of the Little Season.

No matter, their brief courtship in Brighton would soon come to an end. After he returned, their life together as man and wife, or more importantly duke and duchess, would follow before the end of the year.

That very afternoon, Aunt Rose informed Eugenia they were invited to a house party in a week's time at Brookhaven, residence of Lady Penelope, Lord and Lady Coddington. Eugenia was also certain that Aunt Rose had already set her mind to attend and, most probably, had already given their acceptance.

In speaking to Penelope, Eugenia understood that Cynthia, her mother Mrs. Penshurst, and Herr Mueller were also invited. Penelope told them that although her elder brother, Sir Terrence, would not be present, the guests would become acquainted with her younger brother, Randolph.

They would all leave the fair seaside city soon for Surrey. From there, they would remain at Brookhaven until it was time to depart for London.

Eugenia found her life so dull in Brighton without Rothford's company that she was half tempted to begin packing right then.

The following afternoon, while out with Cynthia, Eugenia had a chance encounter the Duke of Rothford. She had no idea he had returned to Brighton.

Her knees wobbled and her heart beat so hard from the shock of seeing him, it felt as if her heart were going to leap from her chest. As she and Cynthia approached, he touched the brim of his beaver and nodded to them as if they were nearly perfect strangers.

Eugenia felt quite dreadful, deeply sorrowed at her lost love affair. How could he have done such a thing?

She expected him to at least slow and greet her. Or perhaps to let a smile grace the cold, chiseled features on what he would, no doubt, refer to as a face.

Especially after his memorable farewell. Eugenia would have thought he'd call, or at least send 'round a note, as soon as he returned from his trip. Obviously she had been wrong about his regard for her.

Before this afternoon's unfortunate incident on the street, she had not seen the Duke for nearly a week. It seemed that not only had her absence not affected him, he did not care that he had seen her by chance.

Perhaps she would ignore him at The Castle assembly, if he should attend. It seemed he felt compelled to attend every social occasion possible. Eugenia was becoming quite cross with him. Rothford treated her in such a horrid manner. He should mind himself or she would hand him the mitten. That is, had they been engaged, which they weren't quite yet. Perhaps she would not accept him when he offered for her. No matter how much he pleaded and begged, she might not accept his marriage proposal. It would certainly serve him right!

Eugenia had no intention of allowing Rothford to ruin her evening. She dressed in her yellow sarcenet gown with a simple string of pearls and met Cynthia at the Old Ship for the monthly full-moon masquerade, the last one before they departed for Brookhaven.

She and Cynthia set their dominos in place. Even masked, it was not hard to tell who was whom after spending the last month among the inhabitants of this fair city.

To her ultimate horror, Eugenia quickly identified the swagger of the man heading in her direction. His eyes glared with their familiar dark intensity. She did not turn away from his accusing stare, but faced it.

Rothford came to a halt in front of her and performed a deep, sweeping bow. She should have had the good sense to kick his leg from beneath him.

"My lady, would you be so kind as to grace a *stranger* with a dance?"

Strangers are we now? Strangers with a tumultuous past, strangers with an uncertain future.

It would be a very strange occurrence indeed if he thought she cared to associate with him after the way he had ignored her.

Eugenia decided it was not a matter of what she wanted. She had the distinct impression he would certainly do as he pleased and would not take no for an answer.

She and Rothford had been the topic of numerous *on-dit* these past few weeks. The duke, on the other hand, did not seem to mind the gossip, or he simply did not know.

She, at least, had the sense to avoid spurring another wave of speculations. So, not wanting to cause a scene, she took his arm.

Her hand tingled at his touch. It spread from her hand to her shoulder and dissipated. How could someone she felt so much loathing for make her feel like this?

Then she realized it wasn't only her. He had felt it too. Even though he was masked, Eugenia could see the effect of their casual contact in his eyes.

He *did* care for her.

Perhaps there had been a valid reason why he had not spoken to her on the street that day. Maybe there was another chance for them.

Here, where it had started a month ago. Here, they might rekindle what they had so sadly lost during his absence and the lonely days that followed. Here, they might rediscover each other.

Rothford took her into his arms as a warm, comforting smile spread across his face. He wanted this reunion as much as she. Perhaps more. Eugenia detected a longing, a loneliness in him that needed healing.

Although she remembered seeing the other guests in a blur of color swirling about her. She could not recall hearing the music as they danced. He pulled her closer, they spun faster and faster.

When they stopped, he politely stepped back and placed a kiss upon her gloved hand. Before he left, he said, "I pray, dear lady, that we meet again."

"So do I," Eugenia replied, playing along. His performance left her in awe that he could so completely remove any doubts she had regarding his affection.

Eugenia stood with Cynthia after they had removed their disguises. "It looks as if you two have settled your differences," her friend commented.

"When it comes to Rothford, I'm afraid I hardly have the willpower to refuse him anything." Eugenia looked back at the double doors where he exited. Barely two minutes later, he returned through the very same as if he'd been away conquering the world.

Immediately Eugenia felt warm, her reaction to that vivid picture in her mind conjured by his presence. She found her escape on the terrace. Part of her needed the fresh air, the remainder secretly wanted him to follow. She wanted to be alone with him.

Rothford did not disappoint. He followed her.

This night rehearsed for the cold winter days to come. Yet Eugenia felt none of the cooling breezes that delicately drifted past her.

He stopped at a respectable distance and bowed his head, addressing her. "Do you think *I* have a chance of gaining a pardon?"

"If I can forgive a stranger, I can most certainly forgive you, Your Grace." Had she not already offered the masked man an apology on the dance floor? Now she needed to pardon the duke as well?

Gradually, he took two steps and closed the distance between them. He ever so slightly tilted her chin with his fingertips. "I do wish you would dispense with the 'Your Grace.' I much prefer that you call me Rothford."

Arm in arm they entered the grand ballroom. For the remainder of the evening, she and Rothford rubbed along together famously. Nevertheless, with their history, Eugenia could not help wondering how long it would last.

She inquired about his plans for the weeks preceding the Little Season. Eugenia wondered if he cared to join her party. She was sure an invitation to the country gathering at Brookhaven could be extended.

However, during the interval Rothford was expected at Claremont Castle, home of the Earl of Claremont, elder brother of his friend, the Honorable Donald Hamby.

Eugenia understood that the duke had certain commitments and she would never dream of interfering. Rothford made her promise him her first dance at Almack's. He also wanted to partner her for the first waltz, when she was granted permission to perform it, in London.

So very much could happen between now and

then. At the moment London seemed so very far away, not in distance but in time.

Eugenia could see how Rothford wished her to enjoy her first, and most certainly her last, London Season as the incomparable. No doubt he believed she should be free to visit the sights and enjoy the attentions and favors of all the desirable young men. The duke must have known all too well that her heart belonged to him.

Tomorrow, Eugenia told him, she and Aunt Rose would leave for Brookhaven. He wished that she should enjoy herself in the country and looked forward to their next meeting in Town.

Rothford led her onto the ballroom for the quadrille. They took their starting position on the floor. The music began. The dancers started.

At the present, Eugenia was in heaven.

Chapter Six

Cynthia and her mother, Mrs. Penshurst, led the caravan from Brighton to Brookhaven the afternoon after the masquerade ball. It had begun to rain by the time Eugenia and her aunt boarded their coach and took their place in line behind the Penshurst transport.

Before departing, there had been some discussion of Franz traveling with Eugenia and Aunt Rose. Eugenia had been spared keeping company with the musician, whom she adored, but would have dreaded occupying the same vehicle for an extended period of time.

He was such a delicate man, probably subject to the damp, and to watch him suffer when there was nothing she could do would have been dreadful. Thank goodness Mrs. Penshurst insisted he ride with them. Eugenia could only sympathize with poor Cynthia, trapped in a coach with Franz for hours on end.

"Tell me, Genie dear, did you enjoy your time in Brighton?" Aunt Rose continued, preventing Eugenia from answering. "I for one believe your stay was more than successful."

Eugenia remembered during her journey to Brighton she had dreamed of a highwayman. Now, a month later, she had no need for fantasies of imaginary rogues, she could focus on her handsome duke. How much she had changed, how she had grown.

"You attended your fair share of balls, made more than a handful of friends." Aunt Rose pointed out what was obvious to Eugenia. "And if I am not mistaken, you have formed a desirable attachment."

"It has yet to be determined if the Duke and I have formed an attachment."

"Really? That is not what I have heard." Aunt Rose busied herself by rummaging thought her bag. "Although he may seem upstanding, my dear, there is something I find disturbing about him," Aunt Rose began. "That duke is not without a blemished past."

"What exactly do you mean?" Eugenia inquired with piqued interest. She had never heard a contrary word about him from anyone. Rather, it seemed he was in great demand among the ladies. *Elusive* they had called him, for none of them could catch his fancy.

"It seems the Duke was not always a duke." Aunt Rose eyed Eugenia skeptically. "At one time, Thomas Mallick was only Lord Thomas, a duke's younger son. His elder brother, Edmund, inherited the title when their father passed away some seven years ago."

"Why are you telling me this?" The tormented tone of Aunt Rose's voice set Eugenia on edge more than the quaint tale. "It is not so unusual that a younger brother should inherit an elder brother's title."

"You are quite right, my dear. I simply thought the story was worth mentioning since you seem to want to know all there is about him." Aunt Rose removed her handkerchief from her reticule. "It seems the circumstance of his succession was . . . It appears to me very questionable."

The manner in which Aunt Rose brought up the entire subject did not seem to sit right with Eugenia and it sent a chill down her spine. Eugenia could think of nothing else after her aunt dozed off minutes later.

Arriving at their destination, Eugenia found the estate of Brookhaven to be large, lavish, and beautiful, ample size to accommodate the guests in complete luxury.

Eugenia settled in a brightly colored, cheerful room next to her aunt's. But no amount of pampering or comfort could distract her from what took place in her heart and in her head.

Her thoughts strayed. She missed Rothford terribly,

and it would be more than several weeks before she would see him again. How would she bear it?

And that *had* to be why Eugenia felt so very unsettled.

The next morning, the house guests met Lady Penelope's brother Randolph. Young Mr. Coddington had been in London this past Season. Eugenia thought him handsome but somewhat nervous, tugging on his vest and the sleeves of his blue superfine coat.

He must have been morbidly shy and somewhat panicked when his sister introduced him to the sizable number of guests who had invaded their home.

The presence of so many people caused him to retreat to one of the small parlors where Eugenia observed he must have succumbed to a fit of the vapors. Or did one call it something else when it occurred to a man?

Mr. Coddington explained to his sister, when none of the guests recalled seeing him in Town, that he was far too withdrawn to ever approach anyone even after being introduced. Thus he remained a stranger to all who crossed his path.

Penelope told them later, after Randolph had excused himself, that he found the whole London social scene to be "horrific" and "frightful." He never wanted to return to Town again.

After the journey to Surrey, the inhabitants of Brookhaven spent more than a week of evenings playing cards, making silhouettes, reading poetry, taking turns playing the pianoforte, and singing.

Eugenia's dear friends Penelope and Cynthia were the worst offenders, encouraging one another to sing cheerful, syrupy sweet love songs. Even with Herr Mueller's magnificent accompaniment, Cynthia's solo sounded only tolerable. It was enough to cause one to go mad.

Finally, Lady Coddington arranged an afternoon trip. Three coaches conveyed the guests into Haslemere, the local town. After some shopping, they stopped for lunch at The Goat and Goblet. When their small group exited the establishment, Eugenia, the first to step out onto the walkway, was almost run down.

The man who nearly crashed into her should have been watching where he was going. She might have given him a proper set down if it had not been for his odd reaction to her.

He stared into her face with complete recognition and exclaimed, "I beg your pardon, Lady Eugenia."

Eugenia, of course, was upset at the mishap but this fellow was not known to her and his apology—using her name—had left her quite speechless.

Then, out of nowhere, the Duke of Rothford appeared and took the distraught fellow by the arm and off they went.

That was not well-done of either of them at all.

"Was that not the Duke of Rothford?" Cynthia

stepped out from behind Eugenia. She was the only other person who was able to catch a glimpse of the duke.

"I believe it was," Eugenia said, still recovering. How strange they should run into each other and how ungracious Rothford had been not to have paid his respects.

It was beyond all things peculiar.

Returning to Brookhaven, Eugenia left the company of the other guests to take a turn about the garden for some air to clear her head. Given the time to mull about what the Duke had said to her before they parted Brighton, she wondered how it came about that he was here?

Then she realized how Rothford's quick reaction removed the young man before he could say anything further to her. The Duke had not remained long enough to see her for himself and could, quite possibly, regret his action.

Then, finally, it occurred to Eugenia that the young man who nearly ran into her was the one she had seen before and heard referred to as Foster.

Ten or so minutes had passed before Mr. Coddington joined her on the garden path. They settled into a comfortable conversation. Apparently he found Eugenia an amiable companion and felt at ease, which led her to ask him if he had heard of Claremont Castle. He told her it neighbored Brookhaven and went so far as to point out exactly the direction.

Rothford probably had no notion the two estates were in such close proximity. Eugenia felt certain if he had known of her presence, the accidental meeting would have had an altogether different outcome. He would have made himself known to Eugenia and lingered in the village for hours, perhaps even joining their party's outing.

No doubt he would learn of her presence from Foster, for she was certain the young man would relay the news of their abrupt meeting. Nonetheless, returning to the house, Eugenia dispatched a note to Claremont Castle and waited anxiously for the remainder of the day, fully expecting to hear from Rothford at any moment.

Eugenia could not remain calm during dinner. She must have been horrid company for the others, taking no more than a bite from her plate. After dining, Mrs. Penshurst asked Franz to treat her guests to several pieces on the pianoforte.

Unfortunately Eugenia was not in the mood to enjoy his performance. Dear Franz's last effort to uplift her spirits was an evening stroll to which she had agreed but cut short, claiming a headache.

That night, Eugenia tossed and turned unendingly, completely unable to sleep. Perhaps if she read something it might help her fall asleep. At least it would allow her to pass the remaining hours until dawn.

She rose from her bed, the chill moved through her thin cotton set and she pulled her wrapper around her neck to keep out the night's air. After lighting a taper and heading down the hall, Eugenia descended the staircase and strolled into the study.

Holding the candle before her, Eugenia saw there, pressed close against the end of the bookcase and casement window, among the drapes, stood a man. A man who was trying very hard to remain invisible.

Eugenia could not believe her eyes when she realized it was Rothford!

She could see the very same surprise and delight in his face when they looked upon each other. Truth be told, he was probably more thankful that it had not been Earl Coddington who had discovered the unexpected presence in his country home.

She set her candle on the table and ran to the Duke with open arms. "You got my message!" They embraced. Eugenia had never been happier to see anyone in her entire life. She was even more elated that he shared her enthusiasm.

"Why do you think I'm here?" His informal attire boasted a further reason why he did not wish to be seen by any other, for he only wore a shirt and breeches.

He must have pretended to retire for the night. Then he leaped out his bedchamber window and dashed headlong through the meadow and into the night to Brookhaven to meet her!

"I am so happy you have come." Eugenia held

him tight, overjoyed to see him. How could she have ever doubted his affection?

"How could I not?" he whispered. A nervous smile crept onto his face. "Although, I admit, I am taking quite a risk seeing you like this."

Eugenia glanced at his attire. It did not offend her. In fact, Eugenia found it quite enticing. His shirt lay unbuttoned around his throat. He took her hands in his, drew her close, and placed a gentle kiss upon her lips.

He was truly the romantic figure from her dreams. How could she not lose her heart at the very sight of him?

"Rothford!" she gasped, realizing their circumstance. "Please! We shouldn't be alone . . . not here . . . not like this!" This was not at all proper. If they were to be discovered, the plans for Eugenia's grand London wedding would be for naught.

As the man of her dreams, he would hold her interests above his own. As expected, he froze at her alarm, realizing what she said to be true, and pulled away.

"You're quite right," he said. "I forgot myself for a moment."

She straightened her thin nightrail and smiled with relief that he understood completely.

"If I should visit again"—he smiled wryly—"perhaps I will act more in line with our stations."

She regarded him in the dim candlelight. It was a

smile he performed when they were alone, only for her, during private moments such as this.

One thing Eugenia had learned about him was that he never allowed that sweet side of him to show in public. Perhaps he thought it too undignified for a duke. That side of him absolutely enchanted her.

"Eugenia, what am I to do with you?" he whispered, tracing her cheek with his finger.

Even though they stood separated by several inches, Eugenia could feel their hearts embrace. They were truly kindred spirits. "I am sure you will eventually discover, given time."

He applied a warm kiss to her already glowing cheek, then made his escape out the French doors, onto the terrace, and into the darkness.

He was truly all wonderful things of which dreams were made. And what Eugenia wouldn't do to feel everything she had just felt again! Her heart pounded, blood surged thought her veins. Every part of her felt so alive when wrapped in his arms.

Perhaps tomorrow, Eugenia mused, she might lose her way during the morning ride and find herself at Claremont Castle.

The next morning the five of them, Cynthia, Penelope, Franz, Mr. Randolph Coddington, and Eugenia, headed out for their morning ride as they had done each morning since their arrival. Reaching the old log by the large oak tree on the hill, the designated return point, they decided to venture out separately and race home.

As planned, Eugenia had an entirely different destination in mind.

The group rounded the large oak tree, turned their horses, and all took different routes back to Brookhaven.

Eugenia headed northeast for Claremont Castle. All she could think of was capturing another kiss from Rothford. No doubt he would be surprised and perhaps cross at first when he saw her. He might even scold her for the impropriety of a lady paying a gentleman a visit. That did not dissuade her, nor did she care.

She felt certain he would be much too overwhelmed with emotion to turn her away. And it was for those few brief, stolen moments they would spend together that she took this journey. After riding at a canter for a good twenty minutes, she heard voices. Loud voices. Men's voices.

Pulling her horse to a halt, she dismounted and carefully moved into the brush to hide. Eugenia remained quiet, although she wanted to cry out when she recognized one of the two men standing in the dew-moistened field before her—the Duke of Rothford.

She said nothing and remained quiet. There was an eerie stillness in the air. Eugenia began to shake, not from cold but from something she could not name.

Perhaps it was because Rothford was not alone. Perhaps it was because he and the other gentlemen were armed.

With the Duke was Foster, the same young man who nearly knocked her down that afternoon a few days ago. Eugenia was certain of it. Foster held a rifle against his shoulder, taking aim in the distance.

"If you don't go through with this, you'll not have the *favor* returned," the Duke ground out, sounding annoyed and impatient. "Come on, man, on with it. You'll never have a better shot at Claremont than this."

Shocked into silence, Eugenia could not, would not, dared not, even if compelled to do so, utter a sound. It was fear. The sudden overwhelming feeling of danger pulsing through her body ordering her not to move.

Several minutes passed when nothing happened. Then Rothford swore and pushed the young man roughly aside. The Duke raised his own weapon and fired without hesitation.

The crack of gunfire that echoed around them was not loud enough to mask Eugenia's scream. Her gelding spooked and bolted, racing out of the bushes in front of the men before heading in the direction of Brookhaven stables.

It was then Rothford faced her. He looked *at* her. She would never forget the dark, hateful glare of those eyes.

Eugenia's vision narrowed into blackness and her

legs gave way under her. She didn't remember hitting the ground. She must have fainted.

When Eugenia woke, she felt disoriented and found herself lying in the center of a small copse of trees. This was completely different from the knee-high, golden grasses of the field she remembered.

"Where am I?" she said, mostly rhetorically.

Someone hushed her. She sat up to see Franz rushing to her side. His presence was totally unexpected. She could not imagine what he was doing here. Even with his poor riding skills, he should have been halfway to Brookhaven by now.

"I saw Rothford kill a man!" she told him, warm tears streaked down her face.

"Quiet! You've got to keep quiet!" he insisted. "I don't know how long we can escape Thomas' detection."

"You don't understand, Franz. I *saw* Rothford deliberately take aim and shoot a man! It was murder!"

Male voices rose around them.

Franz clamped his hand over Eugenia's mouth, silencing her. Her arms flew wildly about in protest. Quite unintentionally, as she struggled, she caught hold of his powdered monstrosity of a wig and pulled it from his head. Eugenia gasped when she saw his head of thick, dark hair.

The pressure of his hand increased ensuring her silence and with a whisper bade her to remain silent.

A few minutes after the voices ebbed, he eased

his hold and apologized for having to take such action. Eugenia apologized for disheveling him.

He helped her stand. "Now's our chance. We must flee to safety!"

"I'm not going anywhere with you!" Eugenia stared at him . . . stared *up* at him.

She was not quite sure how but she could have sworn he stood taller. Franz, she recalled, was her height, almost exactly. But now he showed no signs of a slouch. And there was something else decidedly different about him.

"Where's your accent?" she said, for it had miraculously vanished.

This man was not the *Franz* Eugenia knew. This was a stranger who had emerged from her once dear Austrian friend. One that she thought she had known fairly well.

"This disguise." He gestured down the length of his torso. "I completely understand that my current appearance places me in an undesirable light. It can be explained to your complete satisfaction, I can assure you."

She could not even believe her own eyes. How did he think she would believe anything he had to say? Her once good friend stood before her as a stranger.

"I will be more than happy to give you a full account." A lock of his dark hair fell across his forehead. "But it will have to be later, once we are safe. We shall sit down and have a long discussion over a nice pot of tea. I promise. Now let us go!"

Eugenia crossed her arms and planted her feet, determined not to move.

"You know you can trust me, don't you?"

She had been wrong. There was something very familiar about him. The shape of his face, his eyes, his lips . . . It was then she realized why. This man looked a great deal like the Duke of Rothford.

"How can I trust a man who hides behind the identity of a sweet, kind musician?" she said sharply, wondering if sanity had left the world. "One who passes himself as a genteel Austrian but who is in fact a quivering English coward."

"I'm Edmund," he told her.

At least he had a name.

"Please, if we're discovered, Thomas will have no qualms about killing either of us as he did the Earl of Claremont." He peered between the bushes and hedgerow out to the clearing beyond. "I'm sure they are looking for us—you. Please, Eugenia, we must leave."

What this Edmund said was enough to convince her to follow him. Rothford would be looking for her. She knew it. Eugenia couldn't help but glance around when she stepped beyond the sparse outcrop of foliage that had concealed them.

Eugenia lifted the skirts of her riding habit, which grew heavier by the minute, to trudge behind him.

They spent more than two hours on foot over hard, rocky terrain, travelling too fast to hold a conversation.

After the first hour, Eugenia begged him to stop so she could rest her weary feet. Edmund urged her onward, never giving her an ounce of consideration. The man was simply horrid. She hated him.

Finally, she stopped, dropped the two handfuls of her skirt, and refused to take another step. "Sir, I simply cannot continue." Eugenia blurted through labored breaths. I must stop if only for a few minutes."

Edmund glanced around, perhaps checking for a glimpse of their pursuers. "Look, there's a place just up ahead where we can rest."

Was he headed to some secret madman's lair? Eugenia wasn't sure if she could trust him any more now than when this whole wretched business had started. Once again she moved forward trusting, perhaps foolishly, that a place to sit did indeed lay ahead.

They continued another fifteen minutes to a modest abode just outside a village. Edmund knocked on the door.

A moment later it opened. An old man, in keen observation, saw they were in dire need of rest.

"Please, please, come in," he said, pulling the door open wide. "You must sit for a spell. Bess!" he called over his shoulder. "We have weary travelers who are in need of—" The old man squinted, looking closer at

Eugenia's traveling companion. "Your Grace? *Edmund* Mallick? We thought you were dead—lost on the Continent, I heard tell."

Edmund Mallick? Eugenia remembered Aunt Rose telling her that Thomas had inherited his title through the misfortune of his elder brother.

"It was all a misunderstanding," this Franz–Edmund-person explained.

"Pray, come in, Your Grace . . . your young lady as well." The old man smiled, motioning that they should make themselves comfortable.

"Please, please, welcome, both of you." The old woman appeared with a laden tray.

He led the way into the small one-room cottage, and it wasn't a very large room at that. The house was small, very modest. The occupants, obviously known to this Edmund, gladly saw to their needs.

Franz . . . Edmund . . . whatever name he wanted to use, declined the elderly couple's offer to put him and his female companion up for the night, though Eugenia had never felt more weary and sorely in need of a good rest.

They did partake in a bite to eat and some tea. He did accept their offer of the use of their horse and cart for which Eugenia felt most grateful.

"We must retreat to a safe place, far away," Edmund whispered to Eugenia when the couple had momentarily stepped away. "We need to find a place where Thomas cannot find us. A place where we can regroup and you can fully rest."

Yes. Eugenia wanted to get as far away as she could from Surrey, from Thomas, and from Edmund as soon as possible.

Chapter Seven

Franz-Edmund's will was no match for Eugenia's determination that they return to Brookhaven for some of her belongings. Upon arrival, they saw no one, not the guests, not any of the belowstairs servants were present.

"No matter, we must quickly gather what we need and be off." Franz-Edmund ran willy-nilly toward his room to fetch whatever it was he needed to collect while they were there. Eugenia ran to her rooms to have Katrina pack her bags.

Eugenia dashed into her aunt's room, which was the room before hers. No Katrina. She then ran headlong into her own shouting, "All my clothes! Pack everything!"

Only Katrina was not to be found there either.

Only moments later did Eugenia hear approaching footsteps. Relieved that Katrina had returned, Eugenia ran to the clothespress and flung open the door to choose the garments she wished the maid to pack first.

"I want to take everything!" Eugenia called out to her aunt's returning maid.

"An excellent idea, although not necessary." Thomas, Duke of Rothford sounded more amused than worried at the thought of addressing the eyewitness to his act of murder. "You'll be coming away with me."

Eugenia stumbled back into the furniture, putting as much distance as she could between them. She had no intention of going anywhere with him. But she did not have much choice in the matter.

Thomas grabbed hold of Eugenia's arm and drew her toward him, causing her feet to skid across the floor. She put up a struggle as best she could, making as much noise as possible while kicking and screaming, but was too easily overpowered by him. The tears streaking down her face would not stop, nor could she wipe them away.

No one came to her rescue.

Edmund, she knew, was at the far end of the house, for that was where Franz's room lay. More than likely he would not have heard her pleas for help. Perhaps he had chosen not to act the hero.

Rothford could not have known that Edmund was

in the manor, nor would Eugenia give him away. If the younger saw the elder, it would have complicated matters even further. She could not betray poor Edmund.

Rothford was none too gentle with Eugenia, dragging her down the stairs to his awaiting coach, which whisked them away.

The coach lurched forward, plunging Eugenia back into the squabs where she pressed into the corner to get as far away as possible from Rothford, who sat across from her. His dark eyes were more frightening than she ever remembered.

"Well, it seems you have become more of a problem than you were in Brighton, my dear," he said. His voice was not the warm, soothing tone she had bathed in the Brookhaven library last night. His expression was cold and harsh.

Eugenia said nothing.

"I find it difficult to believe you have no comments to make. It seems to me you always have something to say." He regarded her from under arched eyebrows. "We both know what happened. I am well aware you saw me and I, most certainly, saw you. I have no idea how you came to be there but no matter . . ."

She did not wish to appear completely intimidated and leveled a stern glance at him.

"As you observed, Mr. Foster was not truly motivated to do what he had to in order to secure his title. I had no alternative but to intervene." A sneer, not a smile, crossed his face. "I cannot allow you to bear witness against me, which leaves me with two choices. I give you the option of choosing to marry me or die."

"How gallant of you," she replied. The choice was revolting and he was even more so.

"I prefer not arranging another accident so soon after the tragic death of the Earl of Claremont. Of course, you haven't heard the news, my dear, the earl was killed in a shooting accident on his own estate."

"Is that similar to what happened to your elder brother?" She instantly regretted her words. Eugenia could see the mixture of anger and hatred in his eyes. She hadn't realized until this moment he would, as Edmund had told her, have no qualms about harming her.

"I suppose I could arrange for you to conveniently disappear if you continue to prove problematic." The murmured comment was a thinly veiled threat.

"I have no wish to die," Eugenia whispered, her voice all but gone. She felt tears spring to her eyes but the terror inside kept them at bay.

"I'm glad to hear that, darling." He reached across and patted her knee.

The touch of his hand repulsed her. Eugenia willed herself not to react.

"I believe our marriage will be readily accepted, especially after our very public courtship in Brighton.

I suppose I should thank you for that." He smiled and inclined his head in a gracious nod.

Eugenia could slap Penelope for making her flirt with the Duke in the first place. Who would have ever thought she would be blackmailed into marrying him?

"You were quite relentless in your pursuit. I doubt *I* would have made that much of an effort." He sighed, apparently pleased with how easily his new plan dovetailed with their recent Brighton stay. "There are countless upstanding Society members who can attest to our attachment, making our sudden marriage all the more believable."

He crossed his arms over his broad chest and leaned back against the squabs. The strong, confident, and smooth exterior added to the illusion of a man who was accustomed to getting what he wanted. And in truth, who would stop him?

Their destination, it seemed, was a small village. No, this place was much smaller than a village. A substantial *donation* from the Duke persuaded the local vicar to overlook the reading of the Banns or the need of a special license. Two witnesses were found for the marriage ceremony, the document was signed, then away Eugenia and Rothford went to Taramore, his country estate.

Almost immediately after their arrival, Rothford employed the services of a Mrs. Bennett. "My beautiful bride, you are now Your Grace, the Duchess of Rothford," the duke announced, holding his arm out for her at the ground floor landing. "May I introduce to your new lady's maid?"

The footman who stood sentry outside Eugenia's bedchamber door and had followed her down the stairs only minutes before was nowhere to be seen. It occurred to Eugenia that he had been dismissed and Mrs. Bennett employed, being far better suited as a watchdog for the new duchess.

The woman dipped into a modest curtsy but she did not appear genteel enough for a lady's bedchamber. Eugenia felt certain that this lady lacked the skills to successfully employ curling tongs nor did she know how to lift a stain from Eugenia's favorite muslin frock. Although stalwart and stout in appearance, Mrs. Bennett could use a few lessons from Eugenia's Aunt Rose regarding inconspicuous conduct.

The Duke insisted Eugenia write to her aunt and her parents to explain her sudden absence. He dictated the events of her elopement with the Duke of Rothford and closed the letter with the news they would see her in Town during the upcoming Little Season.

How did he expect to present Eugenia as the happy duchess? She would certainly announce to anyone she came in contact with that he was a complete lying, murderous, wretch. She did not plan to cooperate with him in any way. And if he thought he would have her completely in love with him, acceding to his

every wish by the time they had reached Town, he
was very much mistaken.

Eugenia had the freedom of the house when accompanied by Mrs. Bennett, but the new duchess
was not permitted to leave the grounds. Taramore was
very large, but not so vast she could satisfactorily
conceal herself if she should try to hide from him.
She feared that Rothford knew every nook and niche
on the estate grounds. There was no doubt that he
could eventually find her, probably with great ease.

No, merely hiding from him would not suffice.
Eugenia had to wait and find a way to escape completely from Taramore and from Rothford.

Eugenia avoided the outdoors altogether. If she
were to roam the garden she might not be able to resist the temptation to flee and she knew exactly how
that action would be rewarded. Rothford would have
no choice but to level at her the same weapon he had
used for the late Earl of Claremont.

For the most part Eugenia chose to keep to the
safety of her rooms. Rothford would occasionally request her presence and parade her about. Such was
the occasion when the new Earl of Claremont, Donald Hamby, came for a visit. He appeared entirely in
black, with a black arm band, a pretense that he was
in full mourning. He did not fool Eugenia one bit.

She had learned enough about Rothford's conspiracy that Hamby had "paid his dues" by murdering
one peer to advance a younger son to their family

title. That qualified Hamby to receive the *courtesy* in return.

He was a murderer.

By arranging these accidents, Rothford ultimately profited and accumulated various favors long after the deeds had been done.

They were *both* murderers.

It was despicable, beyond anything horrible Eugenia could ever imagine. How did she ever think this was the man of her dreams?

Rothford and Hamby spoke freely of their plans for the upcoming assassinations, in front of her, which made Eugenia so very uncomfortable. The more she knew, the less likely it was she would ever gain her freedom.

This afternoon's discussion consisted of adding a member to their group of young bloods clamoring to ascend to their family titles. His name, Mr. Randolph Coddington.

Randolph? Lady Penelope's brother! He wanted to arrange his elder brother Sir Terrence's murder so he could inherit? This was incredible . . . impossible . . . Eugenia could not believe this was happening.

Overhearing the Duke and Hamby, Eugenia learned that Mr. Coddington would replace the cowardly Foster, who did not have the mettle for entrée into their elite group.

How the ever-timid Randolph would fair, she could not know. As she recalled, the just-grown boy was frightened of everyone and nearly everything. Eugenia wished she knew of some way to warn the family. No longer was it only her life she feared for, it was Penelope's elder brother's.

There were great stretches of time when she did not see Rothford. The staff was instructed to tell Eugenia he was *away*. She knew exactly what occupied his time while *away* and did not press Mrs. Bennett for any further details.

As was her habit, Eugenia read in the conservatory for several hours during the afternoon. This fine day she sat in her preferred, overstuffed puce chair, for none in this residence were her favorite, and Mrs. Bennett sat at the other end of the room plying her needle and keeping an observant eye on the duchess.

At the hour of three, Dawson the butler brought in their afternoon tea. While handing her a saucer and teacup, he discreetly passed Eugenia a small, folded slip of paper.

Without a word, she slipped it into her book and finished her tea. Taking her time, she read for an hour more to allay any suspicion altering her routine would cause. Eugenia returned to the safety of her rooms for privacy to open the note and read the contents.

The note explained she had not been abandoned and that she should take care in dealing with Rothford. He could and would turn against her at any time, no matter how amiable he might appear.

That was not news to Eugenia. She had witnessed

the Duke's quick change of mood and an explosive temper at the slightest dissatisfaction.

The other bit of information from the missive was that she could depend on Dawson the butler.

Eugenia debated whether she should trust the information in the message and decided she had no other option. But who could have sent the note?

Her Aunt Rose? Had Eugenia's aunt somehow discovered her whereabouts? And was a rescue in the works?

Surely not Franz . . . Edmund.

Edmund was aware of her predicament. However Eugenia could not count on his assistance. If he had any sense at all, he would be hundreds of miles from there, safe and sound.

Rothford would make certain Edmund died a second time if he were to discover his elder brother alive.

But he might have told someone . . . the authorities . . . perhaps he could have left an anonymous tip! Then someone could save her from this dreadful place.

If only someone would.

Nearly a week later, again at tea, she received another note. It said:

I have planned your escape. Meet me in the study at 2 in the morning.

Eugenia realized this might have been a trap. Yet this might be her only chance to flee and she needed to warn the Coddington family.

There was no other choice. Eugenia had to trust the person who sent the missive.

That night Eugenia did exactly as the note instructed. She crept down to the study after everyone had retired for the night, arriving just before 2 in the morning. She wore a traveling dress and cloak, prepared to make her escape.

She entered the library with great caution. To her surprise, she spotted a dim shaft of light emanating between two of the built-in bookcases and falling upon the floor. With a bit of prying, she soon discovered the bookcases were not built-in at all.

It took very little effort to move them apart. The hidden door revealed a dimly illuminated hallway carved from rock. The door latched behind her as she stepped through. She realized then, whether she wanted to or not, there would be no turning back.

She stood silent, listening for any hint that might give her a clue as to who was behind this courageous rescue attempt—or who contrived this ruse to cleverly engineer her demise.

The crush of gravel sounded as someone trudged toward her. Whomever it was must have heard the door latch shut after she entered.

Eugenia held her breath, afraid the sound might be heard. She wanted her heart to stop beating, for fear that it would give her away. She did not know who or what she would find in this great cavernous corridor. The pathway traveled downward far beyond her line of sight.

"Eugenia?" someone beckoned from the dark.

"Who is it?" she returned with trepidation, wishing the voice sounded more familiar. She peered below but it was impossible to see.

"Edmund."

At his answer, she thought two things: either Edmund was the bravest soul on earth or the biggest fool she had ever known. His further actions did not hint as to which was correct.

He appeared before her, holding a small lantern. "We must hurry. We have a great distance to travel and we want to be well on our way before sunrise."

"Why did you not—" She began then switch questions in midthought. "How—"

"There is no time to explain, we must be off." He reached out to aid her deeper into the tunnel that led far below. Eugenia took hold of his outstretched hand and they began their journey.

They spent hours winding through the man-made, cavernous tunnels under Taramore. During this escape, Eugenia did not dare voice fatigue. She would prove tireless for as long as Edmund needed her to continue.

They traveled through passage after passage of

hewn, cold-chiseled rock, framed with old, decaying wood supports. The dank, uncirculated air hung stale and heavy to breathe.

Then Eugenia heard the faint sound of water, not dripping, nor flowing like that of a crisp moving stream. It was the loud roar and crash of waves breaking against rocks. Up ahead she made out the moorings of a makeshift dock.

The welcome scent of cool salt air wafting in from ahead blew against their faces. The ceiling had risen to a grand height, towering over their heads, opening out to the sea far beyond their sight.

"Let us stop here for a few minutes, shall we?" Edmund suggested. Whether he wished to further admire the seascape, take pity upon her, or perhaps take in her precarious condition, she did not know.

"How are you holding up?"

Eugenia could not manage words but nodded and did her best to smile that her condition was tolerable. She huffed and puffed every step of the way behind him, and was most grateful for the respite.

Light from the half moon glittered, casting silver peaks off the wave caps just outside the cave, highlighting the undulating swells rolling toward them.

He found them a place to sit and set the lamp upon the ground near their feet.

Eugenia stretched her ankles and wiggled her toes inside shoes that were not meant for travel of this sort. Nor was she, truth be told.

"What is this place?" She looked around them, still trying to catch her breath. The lamp illuminated very little. Eugenia could not see what lay beyond the end of the dock.

"It's a smuggler's cave. It hasn't been used for a very long time. Unless my brother has recently." From the darkened look on his face, he must have thought it not an unreasonable assumption.

A sharp snap pierced the air, followed by the sound of crunching gravel. Eugenia's sharp glance met Edmund's, both uncertain of the sound's origin, both afraid of the implication that it meant an uninvited visitor. Seconds passed, the crunching grew louder.

Eugenia reached out for Edmund's sleeve and stood with him as he rose to his feet.

"Well, well, look who's returned." Thomas' voice echoed lightly in the cavern. "My word, you're the last person I'd expect to see." He leveled his pistol at them, stopping within firing range.

"Don't you dare hurt Eugenia, Thomas, I'm warning you." Edmund made the slightest shift of his body, placing himself in front of her.

"You're threatening me? You're very brave for a man without a gun. Don't make any hasty moves, Edmund. I wouldn't want to shoot anyone by *accident.*" He gave wild laugh.

The sound of the ocean came in with the tide, growing louder as time went on, providing a background for the pointed remarks the brothers threw at one another. Anger and animosity, hatred and accusations, remarks that had been suppressed for years. All meaningless words to her but clearly full of significance to them.

Eugenia glanced back and forth between the two. She studied how these brothers on the exterior seemed very much alike. Thomas may have stood a bit taller and Edmund's jaw might have been a little wider, but all in all remarkably alike without the benefit of being twins.

"I'm afraid I've only one gun. My duchess and I have already discussed how a premature disappearance of my new wife would look too suspicious. Besides, we already have plans for London. On the other hand"—he shrugged—"no one will miss you, dear brother. You're already dead."

Eugenia glanced at Edmund, who did not show the smallest mote of fear. How could he stand there, so calm, when she was terrified that he would be killed? They both knew Thomas had every intention of doing so.

Thomas waved Eugenia aside with his pistol. "Step away from him." He inched closer and set his lantern on a small, low outcropping of rocks. "Go on."

Cruel, cruel Thomas. Eugenia honestly believed at this point he wanted to see the fear on their faces. She was too shocked to be frightened and could not decipher her companion's expression.

Wasn't Edmund afraid to die?

She released her hold on him and stepped away. Eugenia choked back a cry, wishing she could disobey Thomas' commands but she dared not.

"Must I remind you that it was *I* you have formed an attachment to, not my brother, and it was *I* you've married? Please"—he scoffed—"you don't even know the first thing about him."

But she did know him, not as Edmund but as Franz. The entire time Edmund, as Franz, was in Brighton, Thomas never suspected his brother was alive nor that he occupied the very same town.

Thomas gave the impression that he was a man of standing and consequence. The only true attribute he had was the resolve to kill to keep it all.

"How you two met is a mystery. I expect you to tell me the tale in its entirety tonight, my dear." Again he motioned her to step away from Edmund.

Eugenia sniffed and muffled a sob that distracted Thomas only momentarily. It was enough time for Edmund to kick his small lantern into Thomas' lamp.

At first, the mass of broken pieces flared then the flames burned at a dim, steady glow. Eugenia screamed and ran from the flames spreading across the dock.

The two men struggled in the dim light. Soon she could not discern one brother from the other. The fire spread slowly down the dock ramp toward the surging sea.

A shot rang out.

One of them staggered back. They faced each other, motionless for a few moments before one tumbled over the edge of the dock and fell into the water. A loud splash told the demise of a Mallick brother.

Which one? She had no idea.

Eugenia sank back into a dark corner and wanted to cry out in fright, to scream with pure terror, but she knew the only one to hear her would be *him*.

A foreboding, darkened figure approached. Eugenia could not be certain of his identity in this obscure light. The two brothers looked too similar and it was too dark for her to tell them apart.

She stood motionless and remained quiet. Contemplating her movements, Eugenia would only take one slow, small step toward him, and toward the dock's edge, at a time.

"Come," he said. Whoever *he* was.

She inched closer, wondering if this was the wrong brother bidding her near. Should she follow and throw herself into the icy water below?

Her heart felt as if it had stopped. A lump had lodged itself in her throat. She could hardly swallow.

"Please, Eugenia, don't move." He held his arms out to her. "You're safe. It's me, Edmund."

Edmund . . .

If only there was some way to know for sure. The planks creaked beneath her feet, gave slightly as she shifted her weight from foot to foot.

She was almost too frightened to speak. "How do I know?" she managed.

"Come closer . . ." The figure held his hand out to her. "Look at me."

Eugenia dared not and she took another step toward the sound of the sea.

"*Warten Sie, Fräulein*," he whispered, then in that familiar, soft Franz voice said, "*Darf ich Sie um diesen Tanz bitten?*"

Eugenia's knees weakened, almost preventing her from rushing headlong into Edmund's arms. She collapsed against him, tears of joy and relief ran down her face.

Eugenia had never been happier in all her life to see the face of her friendly Franz. He wasn't Franz anymore but still a familiar face of her dear, dear friend.

"It's all right," he whispered into her hair. He held her close. Wrapped securely in his arms, she held on to him where she felt safe.

With Thomas' death, she and Edmund could safely return to Taramore. Edmund then sent for the magistrate and subsequently Mrs. Bennett was arrested.

Suffering from shock and complete exhaustion, Eugenia gave a statement. Edmund tried to limit her questioning and the need for her to testify. Being one of the victims and the sole witness, it would seem unavoidable. They needed to remain at the estate until the authorities had time to complete their investigation.

Edmund promised her that after this awful business was finished, he would see Eugenia to London and to her family as soon as possible.

It was her dearest wish and all Eugenia could ever want.

Chapter Eight

By the end of the following week, the local authorities had been out to Taramore to thoroughly search the passageway and the hidden dock area that lay below. Thomas Mallick's body had yet to be recovered and might be another victim laid to rest in the Channel's waters.

Eugenia was very pleased that Edmund Mallick had been cleared of any wrongdoing and had regained his title, entails, and family holdings. The poor man lost five years of his own life, spending them hiding from his younger brother.

She saw very little of Edmund, spending most of the week recuperating and resting from her ordeal. Her opinion of him did not change. After all, was he not Franz without the accent?

118

Oh so agreeable and ever so much more handsome. How could she have ever confused the two brothers? Thomas the nasty and cruel could not be further removed from Edmund the kind and amiable.

What Eugenia had difficulty comprehending was how Thomas could have ever misled her into believing he had formed an attachment to her. The affection he displayed seemed so real, so utterly convincing. Even more perplexing was how she could have cultivated any affection for him.

Eugenia could not have been more elated by her current marital status . . . widow. It was unfortunate that the life of a man had to be lost. However, she felt it could not have been a more deserved demise for someone as despicable as Thomas.

Edmund proved to be the same kind of friend to Eugenia as Franz had been. While he sent her ahead to London, he remained behind to handle last-minute details with the investigation, thus sparing her from further distress.

Instead of being delivered to her family's townhouse on South Audley Street, the driver had orders to take Eugenia to the Rothford residence in Hanover Square.

Dawson the butler, transplanted from Taramore, notified her of the full availability of Rothford's accounts for her personal use. Eugenia had no interest in shopping in London. The reason she had wanted to come to Town was to be with her parents.

She shook off her fatigue the next day and gladly took the new duke at his word, making significant purchases at each shop she chanced to visit. Eugenia couldn't help but take her anger out on his pocketbook. On her return, she still felt at odds with the entire housing arrangement.

The staff had orders to keep her occupied until Edmund's arrival. Eugenia could not, even if she wanted to, find her parents' townhouse. To rent a hackney on her own would be out of the question, and she could not walk there since she knew nothing of this city.

Once again she was being held prisoner against her will. Only the keeper had changed, hopefully for the better.

Although her past with Edmund, when he was Franz, told her he could be trusted, Eugenia could not imagine his reason for keeping her detained.

She wrote to her parents, who must have finished with their business in London and returned to Langford House by this time, or perhaps they were on their way to Town at this very moment!

Eugenia directed a second letter to her Aunt Rose. The missive addressed to Earl Coddington's country home Brookhaven, her aunt's last known place of residence. Hopefully the message would be forwarded to her relative wherever she may have gone next.

With nothing more she could do, Eugenia waited, sitting on her thumbs.

Nearing the end of the week, a commotion drew Eugenia belowstairs one evening. Roars of cheer echoed through the house.

There she found the newly arrived duke surrounded by his staff, all tremendously surprised to see him. They thought him dead all those many years ago and were happy to have him returned!

After waiting at least twenty minutes, Eugenia was finally granted an audience by His Grace.

"I must have a word with you immediately," Edmund said, motioning to her to gain her attention.

"I should say so." Eugenia sighed indignantly.

"In the front parlor, if you please," he called to her through the staff surrounding him.

"It's about time." Eugenia could not help sounding snappish, "and do not keep me waiting!" She headed directly to the parlor, anxious to hear what he had to say.

Edmund managed to free himself from his group of well-wishers and soon followed. He closed the doors behind him to ensure their privacy.

"I can't imagine why you found it necessary to extend my discomfort. Why did you not have me delivered to my parents' house as I wished? I do not understand why you had me brought here! Why do you continue to cause me distress? Do you have a good reason? Well, do you? Why don't you answer me?" She glared at him, waiting.

"You haven't given me a moment of silence to speak, my sweet." He paused a moment. Probably to see if she could hold her tongue.

Eugenia proved to him that she could be silent, for not another word came from her lips.

"If you will remain silent and allow me my say, I shall explain the entire affair to your total satisfaction," he assured her.

Edmund explained that the first order of business was to sort through the previous duke's papers. Among the accumulation of documents there was a substantial stack concerning the family's concerns. He searched for detailed information chronicling the more deadly and private enterprise of Thomas' undertaking.

A list of accomplices would have proved most helpful to the authorities in apprehending the culprits. Alas it was not to be found.

It seemed that Donald Hamby, the Earl of Claremont, Mr. Joseph Foster, heir presumptive to Viscount Chelmsford, Mr. Randolph Coddington, and any of the others who happened to be involved with Thomas' conspiracy would all escape prosecution.

Eugenia knew them to be guilty. How their actions could go unpunished was beyond her comprehension.

Edmund continued his tale. During his perusal of his brother's papers he found the marriage document that united Eugenia in holy wedlock with T. E. Mallick, Duke of Rothford. He produced the document in question for her examination.

"This cannot possibly be legal." The document looked familiar. It was the very same vicar's scrawl who had sealed her fate with Thomas Mallick. "I never signed that. Furthermore, I never gave my consent."

"It is not necessary. In Trevithin no one can write. It is customary for the vicar to register the couple's names however he sees fit. In this case, with Thomas' long name and title that followed, he saw fit to use initials."

She glanced at the document and eyed the bridegroom's name. "T. E. I assume stands for Thomas . . ."

"Edward," he said. "However, the very same initials could also signify Terrell Edmund."

"And who would that be?" She felt a chill trickle down her spine. Eugenia glanced at Edmund, who appeared positively granite-faced.

"I was named after our father. He went by Terrell. I have always used my middle name."

Silence ensued again.

"What exactly are you saying?" She dared not blurt out what insane thought had popped into her head. In the first place, it would be impossible. Simply impossible!

"What I'm saying is *I* am T. E. Mallick, Duke of Rothford." His face did not hint of a smile.

Nor did Eugenia's.

"You're not insinuating that *we* are married?" She nearly choked on her words. Eugenia could not have a second unwanted husband. She could not be in the same situation again.

He remained quiet and did not reply. Edmund simply stared at her.

"No! That cannot be." She gasped.

"I'm afraid we are," he said. "Man and wife. Until death us do part."

Eugenia glared at him as if he were worse than the most detested person in the world. At that moment she almost wished he had gone into the ocean with his brother.

Eugenia shook her head from side to side, finding herself unable to utter another word. Unable to comprehend the full meaning of what this meant. There was nothing left for her to say.

"I'm afraid it's all legal. Although I'm not quite sure how it can be." He took the document from her trembling hand. "That is what delayed my arrival." Then he stood as silent as she had been these last few minutes, in a calm that maddened her.

How on earth could he just stand there! Eugenia could not imagine that Edmund would tolerate his happenstance marriage to her. She was absolutely horrified!

To be married against her will was one thing, but to be then bound to a second unwanted husband was outside of enough!

"We could have the marriage annulled." Eugenia wanted, no needed, to believe it would happen. She had to know all this could be rectified, and soon.

"Are you quite sure that is what you want? I do not wish us to act in haste." There was an almost desperate quality to his voice Eugenia could not understand.

"Haste?" She simmered in anger.

He stepped away from her and straightened as if he were about to embark on a lecture or long discussion. "I thought that perhaps if we took time to—"

"This cannot be what you want . . . what either of us wants," she interrupted. "I cannot see that I am behaving in any other way besides a rational one."

A wry smile graced his lips. "I don't think you would feel that way if you knew the entire truth," he tossed over his shoulder. With that, he strode out of the room.

Truth? What *other* truth was he speaking of now? How many secrets could one family have?

That fortuitous afternoon, and it seemed as if it were the first one Eugenia had experienced in a very long time, she received a reply to her first communication to her parents. Her mother informed her that they had only just arrived in Town.

Eugenia immediately wrote to her mother, asking

that her clever Papa should come right away, for Eugenia needed his aid to free her from this current, horrible predicament.

She had thought Papa would have pelted over to Hanover Square on receiving word that his dearest daughter was distraught but, alas, it did not seem so.

It appeared these days she was finding it difficult to trust any man. Now it seemed she was married to the brother of her late husband, which in itself was scandalous!

What of her dreams of falling in love? It was what she had always wished for, dreamed of. The truth happened to be that she was in love with no one. Being a duchess did not make her circumstance any more tolerable.

Eugenia simply could not believe, after all she had been through these many weeks, that she was still away from her family and in such unfortunate circumstances.

Her only wish was to go home and run to her mama's comforting arms. Eugenia had not always been understood but, after all, she was flesh of her flesh, her mother would not be so heartless as to turn her away.

For the next several days, Eugenia sought the refuge and safety of her rooms. She had not heard or seen from Edmund since the day he told her of their unfortunate predicament.

On the third evening Dawson called her down for supper as he had the previous two evenings of her retreat. Eugenia was far from hungry and wanted to share Edmund's company even less.

"His Grace wishes me to convey to *Your Grace* his insistence that you join him for supper."

Your Grace? If Dawson was calling Eugenia *Your Grace* then that meant the entire staff believed she was now the Duchess of Rothford. It wouldn't be long before everyone in London would know.

"You may tell *His Grace* that I have no intentions of joining him."

"In the event *Your Grace* does not wish to appear, *His Grace* has instructed me to inform *Your Grace* that *His Grace* will be happy to take supper in *Your Grace's* sitting room."

"What? Here?" Eugenia was outraged at the depths *His Grace* was willing to stoop. "Very well. Tell *His Grace* I will come down and join him shortly."

What else was she to do?

Eugenia began her hasty toilette. How could she be expected to appear presentable if she did not have a lady's maid? She, alone, could barely manage to brush her own hair, let alone style or curl it. Her gorgeous hair, in which she had always taken so much pride, was an asset only if Marianne, Katrina, or a capable lady's maid could tame the tresses. Here she had no one. Then it came to her.

Perhaps she could simply repulse him. She hoped that a ragged appearance would make him reconsider their current marital status. It was certainly worth a try.

Eugenia brushed as much of the curl out of her hair as she could manage and tied it back with a ribbon. She rummaged through her clothespress, looking for the most dreadful frock she owned.

Drat her exquisite taste! Even her old ones were better than she wished to be seen in. She settled for a plain, simple *jonquille* frock with no embellishments.

Eugenia would make Edmund regret he had asked to share her company. She would display her most atrocious, repelling behavior and devise subsequent ways of causing him as much unhappiness as he had caused her. In a day or two, he'd be racing to be rid of her.

She waited in the parlor. Her heart leaped when Edmund appeared. And she hated to admit how very disappointed she had been in herself.

White cuffs and collar along with a gold trimmed waistcoat made a sharp contrast against the black stock and dark blue set of his evening clothes.

Eugenia could not help but think how much Edmund looked like Thomas. His dark hair, his dark eyes and, she'd almost forgotten, his dark heart.

Her memories of Thomas were not all bad. At the end he had treated her poorly. When she recalled their early days in Brighton, she found the more intimate moments they shared were quite unforgettable and very pleasant. He may have had faults, granted they were overwhelming in number, but she could not deny how he had made her feel.

Eugenia did not know how she could even think about such things now, except Edmund was so very attractive, so very . . . well, that was beside the point. She could make such a cake of herself when a handsome gentleman was about. For she knew he could not be trusted any more than his brother.

Edmund offered her his arm to escort her to the dining room. "How good of you to join me," he said amiably as if she had done so out of free will and not from a threat.

"You didn't leave me much choice, did you?" She placed her hand in his and tried to give him the meanest, hardest stare she could manage.

He ignored the barb and led her to supper. "May I compliment you on your choice of attire this evening? Fashionable, yet comfortable."

Eugenia could not tell if he was serious. He was certainly going out of his way to not provoke her.

"I'm afraid I half expected you to want to go out tonight." He pulled her chair from the table to seat her.

"Go out? In public? With you?" She was appalled at the very idea.

"I can see, my dear, that you have the presence of mind to not rush headlong into anything. It would be expected of us, I suppose, as a newly married couple to spend a certain amount of time alone." He lifted her hand to his lips. "Especially in the early days of our marriage."

Eugenia wrenched her hand from him, stepped back, tripped on the leg of her chair, and landed on the seat with an undignified plop. "The last thing I want is to be alone with you."

"Well, I'm afraid it's only the two of us sharing this large house. It cannot be helped." He sat at the head of the table, took up his soup spoon, and began. "Hmmm, very good. You should try some."

"I'm not hungry, thank you." She pushed the bowl aside and displayed her profile.

"As you wish, my pet." Edmund continued with supper. He did not allow her disinterest in food to deter him in the least. That wretched man!

Eugenia sat there and watched him eat course after course. She touched not a bite. How could he act so normal, so unconcerned, when she felt so miserable and suffered?

After supper he escorted her to the library to sit before the fire while he read poetry to her. It was a pastime Eugenia usually enjoyed but it was not an activity she would wish to share with him.

Again she pulled her hand from his before he could kiss it and without wishing him a good evening, she left for her rooms to retire.

Edmund was taking advantage of what he had learned about Eugenia when he was Franz. It was not at all proper. It simply was not fair.

What an insufferable, dreadful man.

Chapter Nine

What was to become of her? Eugenia pulled off her dress, all by herself, and hung it. She pulled her wrapper on over her chemise and sat by the hearth in her room.

Trying ever so hard, Eugenia imagined she heard her mama's voice, seeking comfort in what she would say in this hour of misery.

Eugenia should have paid more attention to her surroundings. For out of nowhere, or so she thought, came Edmund wrapped in a dark blue dressing gown.

"Good evening, my sweet," he said. He tightened the sash around his waist.

Eugenia leaped up, rounding the settee to place it between them. "How did you get in here?"

"We have adjoining rooms as all married couples

do." He looked calm and quite smug about the entire thing.

"Adjoining rooms?" She scanned down the ornately decorated walls, looking for a hidden doorway. Her eyes must have been as large as saucers.

"Dear heart, I'm sure if you gave me a chance I could convince you that you do, in fact, love me."

"No, you could not be more wrong." She side-stepped, keeping him at the opposite end of the furniture, away from her. "I have no wish to be convinced."

"Please, Genie, just one kiss." He dashed around the foot of the settee.

"I do not want to kiss you." She managed to dodge him. "And do not call me Genie."

"You never seemed reluctant to kiss me in the past." He smiled, reaching out for her arm. She darted away, moving out of his reach.

"Kiss you? I have never kissed you." She felt completely confident in her declaration.

When he was posing as Franz, his powdered wig probably fit too tight. It must have affected his mind. It made him imagine things. She always knew that Franz held her attentions much too close to his heart. He must have had fantasies about her. Ones she did not care to think about.

"You most certainly did! It's not something I'm apt to forget!" He smiled a greedy smile and moved toward her. "Actually, we have partaken in that delight more than several times."

"I'm sure you are quite mistaken." She made another escape around the end of the settee. Eugenia did not know why he continued to press the issue but she knew for certain that she had never, ever kissed Franz.

"In Brighton, the Old Castle Inn at the gazebo. I had only meant to kiss you lightly on the cheek. But you looked so beautiful, staring up into my eyes. Waiting, wanting more. I . . . I'm afraid I simply couldn't help myself." He closed his eyes and smiled.

His expression was quite sickening. How could he describe the actions of his brother? Edmund must have seen them together that night. How else could he have known?

"I would warrant to say you enjoyed it every bit as much as I, dear heart."

"You posed as Rothford?" Eugenia was uncertain whether she felt more shocked or outraged.

"I need not pose. I *am* Rothford." He stood straight, declaring it with pride.

"Well, you weren't Rothford then!" She recalled how odd it was that he had returned and his behavior had been more amorous than only moments before when he had said his first good-bye. The reason for the change in Rothford's nature, if he were telling her the truth, dawned on her. "You pretended to be your brother Thomas?"

"How else was I to discover where he had gone? Only you knew. And it appeared you were more than willing to disclose the information." He took up her hand and stepped closer. "I thank you for your cooperation."

"You purposely tricked me into telling you." Eugenia could only stare at him.

"There was no deception. I had to find out where he was going. I did it to save a life. You knew what Thomas had planned. It was my responsibility to stop him."

"How dare you trick me! How dare you take advantage of me!" She stamped her foot in anger and wished she had stomped on his. "How dare you exploit my affections for your brother! My feelings are . . . private."

"You had no real affection for my brother."

Eugenia pulled her hand from his and dashed to the farthest distance she could manage around the settee.

"The point is *I* am the one you have tender feelings for, not Thomas. It always has been." He inched slowly in her direction. "I am the one who cultivated your affections."

"You are wrong. You do not have any idea what you're saying." With all the circling around the furniture, events were becoming a muddle in her mind. Eugenia soon had problems deciphering who was who, when.

"The night of the masquerade, the first one we attended, it was *I* who spotted you from across the

room. It was there *I* approached you for a dance."
Touching his hand to his chest, he indicated himself.
"At the time I had no idea he was in Brighton. I
wanted to dance with you for selfish reasons. As Franz
I found you utterly charming but only as my true self
could I approach you in an acceptable manner."

"You were the man behind the mask?" Eugenia
wanted to believe he was relating another encounter
he'd seen her share with his brother and weaving it
into a tale where he substituted himself for his brother.
But she could not stop her gaze from gravitating to his
hand. She needed to see if he wore it . . . the same . . .
the gold signet ring.

It glimmered in the firelight and was exactly the
one Thomas had worn. Well, perhaps not the exact
one. She realized Thomas' went down with him into
the water.

"The Penshursts were kind enough to sponsor
me . . . Franz . . . home to England. I returned hoping
to find Thomas and reclaim my title. Not until the
evening of the masquerade did I learn of his presence." Edmund chuckled with delight. "I had no idea
you would be such a relentless pursuer and chase after my brother."

"If he was not truly interested in me . . ." Eugenia
could have sworn he had adored her. Well, there
were times when he seemed to care for her then
there were times when he ignored her. "Why in
heaven's name would he play along?"

"Thomas took his role of duke seriously. Excuse my expression, but Thomas would not be caught dead in a mask. He was too proud of his identity to hide, even for a single dance. He wanted everyone to know who he was."

All this was confusing to Eugenia. What exactly did Edmund mean by all this?

"My brother is . . . was the type of person who loved, no thrived, on attention. You provided him with that attention. Positive attention and much, much more. You are the type of wife he thought he deserved, an earl's daughter, and he did very little to win you." Edmund headed to his right. "In that way you were quite irresistible to him. Had he ever kissed you, he would have known what a truly wonderful, captivating woman you are."

"He *had* most certainly kissed me!" Eugenia professed, again switching direction to avoid his capture.

"I think not, dear heart," Edmund uttered with certainty, fueling her anger. "He might have married and done what was expected of him to carry on the family line. He's always one to uphold his duty. He wasn't a ladies' man. Money and power were more to his liking."

"No, no, you're all wrong about him. You're quite wrong," she said, certain he had no notion of his brother's likes or dislikes.

Edmund *had* to be wrong.

"We shared a most delightful tryst." Eugenia knew,

without a doubt, she and Rothford shared the room with no one. "He crept out of Claremont Castle to meet me at Brookhaven in the middle of the night. He kissed me ever so passionately and he had the good sense to restrain himself. But I could tell he wanted to continue."

"You're quite right, *I* did not wish to stop. Again, I had no intention of kissing you at first . . . but, my sweet, how could I resist holding you in my arms? Stealing just one kiss? You were quite right to stop us. Earl Coddington's study was neither the time nor the place."

"The study!" Unless he was present he could not have possibly . . . She was such a ninnyhammer! "How could you—Are you saying . . ."

"That too, was *yours truly.*" He bowed his head, like an actor accepting gratitude for a well-received performance. "May I remind you that it was *you* who came up with the story of Rothford retiring early and riding across the field to sneak into the manor. That was not a tale of my invention."

"How did you—" She stopped midquestion to ask another. "And just what did you think you were doing sneaking around in the study?"

"The same as you, I suspect . . . looking for a book to help pass a sleepless night." He shrugged. "I did not expect that I should have seen anyone at that time of night—so *Franz*, quite foolishly it seems, dispensed with his wig."

Eugenia drew in a long breath and closed her eyes in disgust. How could she have admitted to Edmund how much she had enjoyed being with Rothford. She had treasured those memories, but Eugenia never wanted *him* to know of her feelings.

"We have always enjoyed each other's company. Now that we are man and wife, I do not see why anything should change between us."

"You arrogant pig!" Eugenia swung at his cheek and he caught her hand.

"This is a habit we will have to break, *Liebling.*"

"Do not call me that!" she scolded.

"Anything you say, my sweet."

"Don't call me that either."

He pulled her into his arms and she felt it—the intensity, the passion, it was there . . . between them.

This was too horrible!

It had been him, Edmund, all along. Eugenia thought she was in love with the Duke of Rothford. As it turned out she was in love with the little heel-clicking, German-spouting, Austrian musician.

How disappointing.

He leaned close and murmured something in German into her ear. Of course Eugenia did not understand nor did she care to. Then the door burst open.

"Thunderation! What the devil's going on here? Eugenia!"

"Papa!" Eugenia cried out, trying to push away from Edmund and out of his clutches.

"We came as soon as we could!" Mama called from the hallway, fast on Papa's trail, to their daughter's room.

"Don't look, Margaret." Papa tried to cover Mama's eyes with his hand but she somehow managed to avoid him and beheld Eugenia in Edmund's arms.

"She's disgraced!" Mama staggered back. Papa helped steady her in case she should swoon.

Edmund took his time releasing Eugenia. She stepped away from him and pulled her loosened wrapper around her exposed shoulders.

"Did you invite your parents, Genie? I would have preferred more formal surroundings for our first meeting," Edmund said with a grand smile and held his hand out to Papa. "You must be Lord Langford. Edmund Mallick, Duke of Rothford."

Papa glared at the proffered hand and ignored it.

"Your summons has come too late, Genie," Mama sobbed. Tears sprang from her eyes.

"Oh, no, Mama. You've come just in time." Eugenia rushed to her mother's side.

"Have you forgotten, *Liebling*, we were amidst the throes of passion when your parents interrupted."

"No, no, you're wrong. There were no throes, no passion." She shook her head. "Mama, please I want you to take me home with you."

"My dear, you cannot have been more compromised." Her mother looked at her in that serious manner Eugenia always hated. The one that always dashed her dreams and brought her back to the world she did not wish to face.

Edmund smiled and straightened his dressing gown.

With a cry, Mama fainted. Papa and Eugenia led her to the settee.

"I ought to thrash you on the spot!" Papa roared at Edmund. Eugenia had never seen her father so angry.

"Thrashing your son-in-law is bad *ton*, my lord."

"Son-in-law? Ah, yes." After Papa took in Edmund's noble countenance, he swung his gaze in his daughter's direction. "Eugenia, correct me if I'm wrong. I thought you married a *Thomas*."

"Well, you see it's like this, Papa," she started. Mama opened her eyes and sat up just in time to hear the explanation. "Edmund's brother Thomas forced me to marry him. But now Thomas is dead and it seems the marriage license is unclear on which Duke of Rothford I have wed, so now I'm married to Edmund." She looked into her father's face, hoping just this once to find understanding. "You will help me get out of this, won't you, Papa?"

His face remained blank. When she had finished he turned to Edmund and exclaimed, "Thank God you're married then." Papa sighed. He took a seat next to Mama and rested his head on his hand.

"Oh, Papa, no!" Eugenia turned to Mama for sympathy. "Please, Mama, say something."

"Your father's right, dear."

"No. I don't want to be married to Rothford," Eugenia cried, begging for their aid.

"Only moments ago were you not telling me how you delighted in my embrace?" Edmund chimed in.

"You stay out of it!" she snapped. Eugenia turned back to her parents, who had for so many years misunderstood her and prayed that now they would see reason. "Please? Will you not do something?"

Mama took Eugenia's hand in hers. "Genie, dear, think of your reputation. Think of the scandal this would bring the family. Think of your little sister. How will she ever make a successful match?"

What could Eugenia do? Mama was right. Eugenia felt very sorry. In her selfishness she hadn't thought of how this would affect dear Marguerite when her time came to marry.

It was then Eugenia recognized her fate. She knew without Edmund's consent or help from Papa to free her, her situation would not alter.

To her ultimate shock, Edmund and Papa were heartily shaking hands, laughing and clapping each other on the back only moments later.

"Welcome to the family, Rothford." Papa was all smiles and Mama dabbed the tears from her eyes. Only now she was smiling as well!

"Best for all concerned, Langford." Edmund flashed Eugenia a smile and winked. "I promise to take good care of my new duchess. She will want for naught."

"A duchess." Mama sighed and once again applied her lace handkerchief.

"You're taking on a big responsibility, man. And smite me if you ain't the one to do it!" Papa gave an ardent roar and clapped Edmund on the shoulder.

Don't tempt me, Papa.

Edmund rang for champagne. There they were, Mama, Papa, Edmund, in his dressing gown, and Eugenia, in her chemise and wrapper, with champagne celebrating her marriage in her bedchamber.

Mama and Papa left two hours later and Edmund saw them to the door. Eugenia took that opportunity to bolt her door and push her trunk as well as any piece of furniture she could manage in front of the adjoining door to their rooms.

When Edmund returned, she could hear the knob rattle as he tried the door. Then she heard him chuckle. She waited for him to push his way through the barricade she'd constructed, fearing that it would not hold, but she did not even hear him make the attempt.

When she woke the next morning, Eugenia thought last night all a horrid dream. That was until she spotted the two empty champagne bottles and the three discarded crystal glasses along with her untouched glass sitting on the low table in front of the hearth of her bedchamber.

After thinking over the events of last night, she came to the conclusion that she had been totally abandoned by her parents. Eugenia had the strangest feeling that Papa might have felt even relieved to be rid of her, and Mama, her dramatics aside, was pleased to have her daughter elevated to the position of duchess with a duke as a son-in-law. Did she not have any compassion for her own daughter?

There was no tea tray to welcome Eugenia that morning, nor could there have been since every doorway was successfully barricaded. She slid out of bed and had to dress herself. Needless to say, her toilette was vastly incomplete, but why spend hours on end to beautify oneself when there was no one to appreciate the effort?

After washing her face, she brushed the tangles out of her hair, bound it with a ribbon, and donned her green-sprigged muslin before venturing belowstairs.

She tried to step as lightly as she could and hoped Edmund was still asleep. If she were tremendously lucky, he might be out and about on the city streets doing whatever it is he did in the mornings. Were the gaming hells open at this hour?

Eugenia carefully rounded the corner of the breakfast room and cursed her ill luck to find Edmund already seated at the table, just finishing his meal. He launched to his feet and headed in her direction.

"Good morning, my dear, come in. I was hoping to see you before I left."

Fustian, that meant she had only missed avoiding him by a few minutes.

Edmund took hold of her hand so she couldn't escape and used it to draw her near. Eugenia leaned back, retreating from him as far as she could. She felt relieved when all he did was place a light kiss on the back of her hand.

"I know you only drink chocolate in the mornings but you really should eat something, you know. Last night you didn't touch a bite." He led her to a chair and sat her down like a helpless child. "Mrs. Robertson, the cook, has outdone herself this morning."

Since Eugenia hadn't yet uttered a word, Edmund kept talking.

"We have the matter of deciding which invitations we should accept, my dear." He retrieved a basket filled with them. "Gad! I can't believe so many have arrived so soon. Everyone wants the new duchess to appear at their party! Although I can hardly blame them!" Then he set the whole lot of them next to her. "We should choose only the ones you wish to attend."

"We?" Eugenia became very interested at the thought of attending parties but to attend with *him* was another matter completely.

"The duchess cannot very well appear without her duke, now can she?"

She would certainly like to try. But Eugenia did not

voice her thoughts aloud. Her newly acquired ranking
did make her welcome in the highest Society circles.
She'd be welcomed by a new group of peers, flying
higher than she could ever have dreamed. She was
certain Edmund knew full well this lifestyle would be
irresistible to her and he was planning to use it to keep
her content.

Eugenia had to admit he was very clever, very
clever indeed.

"Your parents are expecting us for supper Satur-
day night and I've taken the liberty to accept Lady
Jersey's invitation for a ball for next Monday. Is that
agreeable to you?"

How delighted Eugenia was to hear this. Truly
something she could look forward to. Life as a
duchess was beginning to sound splendid.

"Charming people, your parents. Your mother is an
absolute angel. I see where you get your stunning
looks, and your father," Edmund chuckled, "one
peach of a fellow."

"Oh, yes," Eugenia said but did not wholly agree.
"A peach."

He retrieved a cup and saucer for his bride from
the sideboard. Without asking, he poured chocolate
for her.

Again, probably without knowing he was doing so,
he took advantage of knowing her habits. He fetched
her toast and placed upon it a dollop of jam, knowing

that was all she ever ate for breakfast, if she had anything to eat at all.

Perhaps she would force an egg and several slices of ham down just to prove him wrong. So she did. Eugenia strode to the sideboard and filled a plate, adding a heaping spoonful of potatoes to really set the thing.

She took a bite of ham.

"I did not realize you ever had such a voracious appetite in the morning." Edmund just stared at her like a hungry cur, waiting for her next word or next forkful of food.

Just for good measure she placed a heaping spoonful of ham and egg into her mouth and sliced another substantial portion on her breakfast plate. "I suppose you don't know me as well as you think you do."

That should show him.

That afternoon brought Eugenia's abigail, Marianne, and three trunks, filled with her clothes and fripperies, to 17 Hanover Square. She supposed Mama and Papa had sent her away in proper fashion now. At least with Marianne's arrival, Eugenia could hold her perfectly coifed head high as duchess.

In her young and foolish youth, Eugenia did not realize the consequences of having everything her heart desired. Nor had she ever thought she would truly have the position she craved and a heroic man who would come to her rescue. It all sounded very romantic but in reality it was far from that.

Thinking over Mama's and Papa's impromptu visit, Eugenia believed Dawson had instructions to allow them entry to witness the entire event, which may have been orchestrated by her feckless husband.

For all she knew he might have sent his own carriage to bring her poor, unsuspecting parents to his townhouse to surprise them! And then again, perhaps her poor, unknowing parents, or perhaps her father, had been involved in the whole scheme from the beginning and waited outside her door for the right moment to step in!

That afternoon, Edmund met Eugenia at the bottom of the stairs and led her to the library. Even though he had given up his Franz persona, she noticed many of his mannerisms were the same. More subdued, but still recognizable.

The series of wide-eyed, enthusiastic gestures told her he was quite pleased with himself for something he had done, or was it something he was about to do?

"My dearest, I've the most wonderful surprise for you," he said, barely containing his glee.

"You've changed your mind about the annulment?" She brightened, hopeful it could be true.

"You wound me, my sweet." He feigned a look of hurt. "I've sent for the Rothford jewels. I know how much you enjoy sparkling gems. They should be here this evening."

"Oh." Eugenia sighed, disappointed. "Yes, I do. Thank you, but I would rather not wear them."

"Appearing with the Rothford jewels will be confirmation enough that you are the true duchess."

Exactly. That was the precise reason Eugenia did not want to appear adorning them.

"Everyone will expect some bauble on your finger." Edmund insisted. "After all, you are married to a duke."

"Thomas never even gave me even the simplest of wedding bands." How truly married was she if she could not claim even that?

The fire in Edmund's eyes flared at the mention of his late brother's name. "I wouldn't want you wearing his ring. I'd have it melted down and sold for scrap." Edmund stood and began to pace. "It truly saddens me, Genie. I have tried everything to woo you. Nothing seems to work."

Eugenia remained quiet. He could go on thinking along those lines forever as far as she was concerned.

"You seemed to like me much better as Franz Mueller. Shall I dress in gold brocade and don the powered wig?" He hunched in the Franz-like stance and toddled around shaking his head, mumbling in German in Franz's voice. Edmund looked ridiculous and she laughed.

It seemed so very long ago, Franz and Brighton. The image of the musician came to mind. He was so odd, so silly, so wonderful.

Franz her ally, Franz her friend.

Edmund *was* Franz, she reminded herself. Why did Eugenia find that so hard to believe?

As Franz, he had provided friendship, companionship, constant comfort, and a shoulder to lean on. Not to mention saving her life . . . twice.

On the other hand, Edmund had used her to gain information about his brother, Thomas, and lied to her a countless number of times.

That afternoon Eugenia received a letter from her mother. In it Mama encouraged her to remain with Edmund and face their difficulties to a passable end.

Her mother was of no help at all. What did being a duchess truly mean if one's mother was constantly dashing one's plans and pointing out one's place?

Chapter Ten

Before Eugenia had finished her evening's toilette, the Rothford jewels arrived. In the small chest were an elegant matching set consisting of large sapphires with smaller diamonds and pearls in coordinating tiara, necklace, bracelet, brooch, and ring. They were grand beyond her imagination. Eugenia thought perhaps there might be a more deserving duchess than she to wear them.

She wore the white satin gown with the French lace. Now that she was married, she did not need to wear white, meant for her London Season debut, but it would be regrettable to allow it to hang in the clothespress unworn.

She sat at her dressing table while Marianne styled her hair. Eugenia opted to wear the simple golden locket her aunt Rose had given her. It was very modest, especially compared to the Rothford family jewels.

She looked upon her fine reflection in the dressing table glass, fingered the locket, and thought of Aunt Rose. Where was she now and what was she doing?

Just as Marianne finished and left, closing the bed-chamber door behind her, a knock at the door announced Dawson with a letter.

Eugenia opened the missive and it did not come as a surprise that it was from her aunt Rose. The woman was absolutely amazing. She wrote that she was off to Bath. Was that not just like her? When everyone flocked to London, she headed in the opposite direction.

There was no mention of Eugenia's abrupt departure from Brookhaven or the subsequent letter she had written upon her arrival at Rothford House. None of it seemed to worry her aunt. What would she have done if she had known her niece had been kidnapped?

Marianne came bolting into the room.

"Your Grace, your aunt is here."

"Aunt Rose?"

"Yes, Your Grace. Mr. Dawson has placed her in the drawing room."

But how . . . so soon? Eugenia had just received her letter. How was it possible? She gathered her skirts and rushed off to see the lovely, elderly relative.

Aunt Rose was real. Eugenia saw her with her

very own eyes. What she found even more surprising was that she had apparently broken up a positively intimate coze between her and Edmund. What could they possibly have to say to each other?

"My sweet, your aunt is here, isn't this wonderful?" Edmund proclaimed.

Eugenia did not know why but he did not seem surprised by her arrival.

Aunt Rose opened her arms wide to greet her niece. Eugenia moved toward her and they pressed cheeks in welcome.

"I'm so glad to see you looking well, Eugenia," she said.

Eugenia felt horrid. "I suppose I'm baffled at your presence. I only just received your letter saying you're off to Bath."

"Of course, I am off to Bath, my dear Eugenia. I'm just taking the route through London." Aunt Rose circled her niece as she spoke.

Eugenia was not sure if her aunt was inspecting the result of her toilette or observing her condition as a whole.

"You left Brookhaven without a proper good-bye." She glanced at Edmund. "Can you blame me for worrying about your welfare?"

"I do apologize for my abrupt departure." It wasn't as if Eugenia had a choice with Thomas Mallick dragging her off. "I did send a note."

"Yes, yes, and His Grace, here, also sent his

personal reassurance that you were well." Aunt Rose embraced Eugenia lightly and patted her on the back in the most affectionate way. "I must admit some confusion regarding the whole incident."

"Mrs. Templeton tells me she'll be staying with us for a few weeks, if that's all right, my dear," Edmund interrupted. His eyes stared at Eugenia, bright and wide.

"That is wonderful." Nothing could have made her happier. She was in dire need of the company of a *loving* family member. "Only now I'm afraid we're off to Mama's."

"I understand, dear, do not give it another thought. You and Edmund go right ahead, by all means enjoy yourselves." Aunt Rose tugged at her gloves, pulling her hands free.

"I cannot leave you behind like this . . . not alone." Eugenia began to regret their evening plans.

"Do not think of it as leaving me behind. Give your mama and papa my best and do beg their forgiveness for my absence—simply mention that I have been traveling." Aunt Rose smiled one of her most pointed, knowing smiles. "The day has been a long one for me. I am fatigued from my long journey and wish only to rest. They will understand."

Aunt Rose followed the housekeeper, who led her toward the stairs to take her to her rooms.

"I will see the two of you in the morning. Have a

good time, my dear." She looked around her niece, at Edmund, and winked. "You too, Your Grace."

Eugenia's mind was in a muddle. Her aunt's unexpected arrival had baffled her. Going to Bath through London? Ridiculous, even for Aunt Rose.

"We should be on our way," Edmund said from somewhere behind her.

Dawson brought Edmund's hat, gloves, and coat. Edmund held a fur-lined cloak to drape over Eugenia's shoulders.

"That's not mine," she stated, stepping away from the expensive outerwear.

"Yes, it is. It's my gift to you." It was a lovely dark gray with soft white fur, lining, and trim. "I can't take a chance you'd catch a chill."

Chilled? He created more chills down her spine than she could have caught had she run through the dead of winter stark naked.

"Very well." Eugenia turned, allowing him to drape the cloak about her shoulders. She could feel him near. His warm breath caressed the nape of her neck, and she held her breath with dread, with fear, no . . . with anticipation, of Edmund's soft kiss.

"I hope you are pleased with it," he said simply without any of the terms of endearment he usually added.

She faced him and caught a peculiar look in his eyes. It left her with a very unsettled feeling. Without a word, he helped her board the carriage.

They arrived at South Audley Street and he escorted her to the front door of her parents' house, where she was welcomed not as a returning daughter but as a ranking member of Society.

The greeting was restrained, cool, not at all what Eugenia had expected. She had hardly recovered from her earlier surprises of the evening when she was faced with yet another. Her dear friends Miss Cynthia Penshurst and Lady Penelope Coddington were also in attendance.

The three young ladies fell into one another's arms in screams of joyous rapture. It seemed Edmund was responsible for this delightful reunion, Cynthia and Penelope told their friend, the new Duchess.

With tear-filled eyes, Eugenia stared at her husband, knowing mere words could not express the gratitude she truly felt. He returned a small, polite smile on his blurry face.

Eugenia led Cynthia and Penelope to the front parlor and left Mama and Papa to fawn over their new son-in-law.

"Oh, Eugenia, I can't tell you what a relief it is to see you well," Cynthia began.

"Cynthia, Genie's more than *well*, she's a duchess now." Penelope winked, sounding more than pleased for her friend.

"Your Grace!" they chorused and dipped into a deep curtsy before breaking into unbridled laughter. Cynthia and Penelope grabbed onto each other, nearly toppling over.

"Oh, stop it!" Eugenia scolded them. "I'm still the same. I haven't changed in the least."

How she wished she could return to that time when the three of them were in Brighton, having the most enjoyable time imaginable, acting silly and giggling over the smallest amusing detail at the local assembly.

"How can you possibly be *the same*, Genie?" Penelope sent a lingering look out the parlor door toward Edmund, who looked quite dashing in his evening attire. "The duke is so very handsome. I'm quite sure his *love* must have somehow changed you."

Cynthia followed Penelope's gaze out the door, making her own observations. "He has such smoldering eyes, and wonderfully strong broad shoulders . . . I am sure it could cause one to—" She stopped and took a deep breath, fanning the rising color in her face.

"We know that you would never have married him if you weren't completely in love," Penelope whispered.

"Yes, Genie, tell us how it all happened?" Cynthia had learned her overeager curiosity from the hours she'd spent with Eugenia, most likely.

"Yes, tell us how you two fell in love!" Penelope urged.

The two friends giggled then sighed at the very thought of Eugenia and Edmund's mutual affection.

Were she and Edmund in love?

"Oh, Eugenia, it's only that we're quite jealous of your good fortune," Cynthia purred.

Eugenia would not claim anything that had happened to her this past month as with the words *good fortune*. She led her friends to the striped sofa where they sat hand in hand in hand.

"When you did not return to the house after we had split up, we were terribly worried," Penelope said. "You remember, after our morning ride? We meant to race back to the stable. Your horse came back to the barn riderless."

"We were so worried and we did not know what to do."

Eugenia could see the concerned, anxious look on Cynthia's face.

"My parents were on their way to town with Lady Coddington and your aunt Rose. All the guests searched for you. We had the servants out, helping us look for you."

Now Eugenia understood why Brookhaven had been empty. She had wondered at the time where the staff and all the guests had gone, and why it was no one heard her cries for help.

"If it weren't for Franz's poor riding skills, we would have never known what happened to you," Cynthia sighed.

"Franz?" Eugenia managed. But Franz-Edmund had been with her.

"Did you not know? It was such a trial for him to sit atop a horse. It took him forever to return to the house. He told us he saw you leave with Edmund." Penelope glanced toward Cynthia as if to check that she had the facts correct.

"Did he, now?" Eugenia looked from Penelope to Cynthia, thinking what an odd thing it was for him to have said.

"You most probably never saw him." Cynthia shrugged.

"Franz said he had taken a tumble off his horse on the other side of the stream, you see," Penelope explained.

"He said he felt safer if he walked his mount back to the stables. To tell the truth I think the poor dear was afraid of horses," Cynthia told them in confidence.

"The tall shrubs and trees probably hid his approach," Penelope continued. "He hadn't meant to eavesdrop, of course, but had he moved, he might have spoiled *the* moment."

"Ah, yes, *the* moment," Eugenia echoed, wondering to which moment Franz with his very active imagination had referred.

"He told us how romantic it all was." Penelope sighed and gazed heavenward.

"Was it? Romantic?" Eugenia believed it was then

she began to feel ill. How could her friends think such a thing when they could not have been more wrong?

"Oh, yes," Cynthia fantasized, a dreamy expression crossed her face. "After years away from his country, Edmund, the returning Duke of Rothford, was determined to reclaim his title. However, once he laid eyes on you he fell desperately in love."

"He first saw you in Brighton, you know." Penelope informed her. "Edmund couldn't allow Thomas to take you away as he had stolen the title, years before. He learned that you were to go to Brookhaven and followed, staying in nearby Haslemere."

Cynthia went on, "Franz overheard the duke—Edmund—say that he did not wish to make his presence known to the others and meant for you alone to see him so he could explain his circumstance."

"He has such high admiration for you." Penelope sighed again. "It was so very wonderful."

The entire scenario was so very silly.

"Edmund watched us ride off in different directions as we raced home." Lady Penelope blinked. "Then he began his pursuit while you were alone. He said that it was very difficult to gallop his horse up to yours. He was surprised that you were such a bruising rider."

It was all Eugenia could do not to choke at how ridiculous that story sounded. A bruising rider, indeed!

"He expressed his undying love for you. He wanted you to run off and become his duchess!" Cynthia sat forward.

"Then the two of you returned to Brookhaven while everyone was out searching. You took only a few of your things and left with the man you love." Penelope's breaths came and went in gasps.

Eugenia thought she might expire on the spot.

"Oh, Genie, what is it like to have a man express his undying love to you?" Cynthia gushed, staring at Eugenia, waiting for her answer.

"Well . . ." Eugenia had to think about what she would say very carefully. "It wasn't exactly undying love he was expressing to me."

"I hear he wanted to marry you that very day." Penelope went on with certainty.

"He wanted to lay his entire dukedom at your feet." Cynthia honestly believed every word of Franz-Edmund's outrageous tale.

Eugenia tried to inject some sensibility into this conversation. "I cannot in all good conscience admit that any of what you say is—"

"It was a love match." Penelope sighed and squeezed her eyes tight.

It was perfectly clear to Eugenia they hadn't heard a word she'd said. Their minds were already grasped on to the ridiculous notion that she had taken part in the most romantic epic of the decade.

It was then the dinner gong sounded and they left

for the dining room. It was a good thing too. Eugenia did not know how much more gammon she could have taken.

Eugenia hardly touched anything on her plate. With all the talk of her elopement, Franz, and true love, she wasn't very hungry. After the meal, Cynthia, Penelope, Mama, and Eugenia removed to the parlor, leaving Papa and Edmund to enjoy their port.

"I can't believe you're married to a duke." Penelope drew in a breath and held it, starting the whole wretched business again.

"But he isn't the same duke you set your cap for in Brighton, is he, Genie?" Cynthia asked with a tilt of her head. She lowered herself onto the sofa next to Penelope.

Eugenia saw the scandal trying to raise its ugly head. She had agreed to stay married to Edmund to prevent gossip and disgrace. Before her eyes, Eugenia's friends were in the midst of revealing her involvement in a matrimonial triangle.

"No," Eugenia answered. How was she to word her side of the story? How much of the truth would it be safe to tell? Eugenia decided to tell them as little as possible without lying.

"Edmund is Thomas' brother. Elder brother."

"Oh, I see, Genie. You found out Thomas wasn't really a duke and decided to go after the bigger fish." Cynthia giggled and playfully patted her arm.

"Isn't that just like you?" Penelope chuckled. They both had a good laugh.

Instead of growing angry, a relieved Eugenia allowed her two friends to go on believing that Banbury tale they'd told her. If that was the story they could easily accept, so much the better.

"It was love at first sight," Edmund said, coming into the drawing room, reinforcing her friends' nonsensical notions and silencing any further questions with his timely presence. And none too soon as far as Eugenia was concerned.

He stood by her side and gave a longing gaze with a few heartfelt sighs, which seemed in line with the romantic saga. Apparently it was enough to convince the guests.

"It's all so wonderfully romantic." Cynthia clasped her hands in front of her and gazed at Edmund as if he were some type of fantasy prince. She stood and strolled over to the pianoforte and glanced at Eugenia. "Let's do sing something!"

"I'm afraid I cannot possibly." Eugenia could not tolerate a round of sickeningly sweet love songs.

Cynthia rounded on Edmund. "Do you play, Your Grace?"

"I'm afraid I am not that well-versed at the instrument," Edmund lied with a frighteningly calm expression so as not to give himself away.

Eugenia choked. "Excuse me." He must have

thought the less he had in common with Franz the better.

"It's a shame that Franz is not here to play for us," Cynthia lamented, dropping her wistful smile if only for a moment. "He accompanied me so wonderfully on the pianoforte."

"Where *is* Herr Mueller?" Eugenia made sure not to gaze at Edmund when she asked.

"Oh, Franz went back to Austria. I believe he's received a commission for an opera. He was very excited." Cynthia flipped through the music but paused to contemplate. "It was all he could do to relay what he'd seen to us, regarding you and Edmund. Then he packed and left."

Lady Langford, Eugenia's mother, strolled in and agreed to play for Cynthia, who sang her romantic ballads with heartfelt sentiment.

Eugenia at once realized the reasons for Edmund's lie. It must have been to prevent his ex-benefactress' daughter from taking to song. Eugenia had remembered Cynthia's vocal ability as above average but that may have been because her accompanist, Herr Mueller, a superb musician, improved her singing.

Penelope joined Cynthia for the next several songs and their soprano voices blended in a pleasant mélange. Eugenia caught Edmund studying her while the music filled the room. His expression was almost puzzling.

The Duke and Duchess of Rothford looked on as

Eugenia's father, Lord Langford, strolled in, feeling quite jolly indeed. He was the proud father-in-law, and had perhaps a touch too much port, as he added his full, rich baritone to the two lovely young ladies' melody. Then Eugenia's mother, from the keyboard, joined the trio with her soprano trill for the grand finale of the evening.

Chapter Eleven

In the days that followed dinner with her parents, Eugenia did not hear the sound of Edmund's sweet voice nor any of his kind words. She must have done something utterly horrible. Eugenia was quite certain that she had driven Edmund to abandon her.

And worst of all, she felt she must have done the unthinkable and hurt his feelings terribly when he had been all things kind and considerate.

Aunt Rose has been so kind as to keep her company but Eugenia dreaded what would happen when her aunt took her leave. For without doubt, Eugenia would be completely alone and miserable.

Eugenia had come to discover that she did not care a fig for the elegant townhouse, the Rothford jewels, or her new position in Society. What she did care about was sharing Edmund's company. She had hoped to see him that morning but met Aunt Rose in the breakfast room instead.

"What is it, my dear?" the elderly woman asked her niece. Aunt Rose must have read the disappointment written across Eugenia's face.

"He's not here," Eugenia exclaimed, dismayed by her discovery. "I was hoping to see Edmund this morning." She knew tonight they were to attend Lady Jersey's ball and she would definitely see him by then. Still, the thought of spending another day without seeing him was nearly too much to bear.

"He's off attending the Prince's levee," Aunt Rose informed her.

"How fortunate for him." It was an honor bestowed upon a select few.

"Come sit down, dear." Aunt Rose motioned to the seat next to her. "I can see you are troubled."

"Oh, Auntie, what am I to do?" Eugenia sank onto the dining room chair and began to cry.

"About your husband?"

"Yes, Edmund." She blotted the tears from her face.

"Matters of the heart are often difficult, Eugenia. Was it only months ago you thought you were in love with his brother, Thomas?"

Eugenia stopped crying and sniffed. It was a horrid thing to say. She couldn't see Aunt Rose's face through her blur of tears. But of course her aunt couldn't know about what really had happened. Or could she?

"Well," Eugenia tried to explain. "I only *thought* I was in love with Thomas but I have since discovered that I had loved Edmund all along."

"Ah, then it is a good thing you married Edmund and not Thomas, is it not?" She smiled up at her niece as if she already knew the truth. "I would imagine it might prove difficult to set things right again."

Eugenia stiffened, probably visibly.

"You are lucky in that respect, my dear. I see how your husband looks at you. He is certainly a man in love." She took up her tea.

"Do you really think so?" Eugenia blotted the last of the moisture from her face.

"I have no doubt. All you need do is let him know your true feelings and I'm certain he will run to you and never leave your side." Aunt Rose sipped from her cup. "I see that as the only option or you might very well lose him."

"Lose him?" The words shocked Eugenia. She had not thought it would come to that. She had asked him to end their marriage and he could have agreed, but to keep her as wife then all but abandon her made no sense.

"It is a question of declaring your love. If he does not know you share his affection, he may do as you ask and give you the annulment you so desperately want."

Eugenia no longer wished for an annulment. She only recently realized that without her darling Edmund, she was not truly happy.

"You are very dear to me and I must say Edmund appears more than amiable. However unorthodox your marriage, it appears you have made a most fortunate match."

"Oh, Auntie, I believe I have behaved abominably to him. I have been nothing but difficult and contrary," Eugenia admitted. And saying it out loud somehow made her feel worse about her deeds. "I have blamed him for anything and everything that has dissatisfied me."

"Do you believe you were wrong to do so?"

"Yes," Eugenia answered with a sigh.

"It is early in your marriage yet. There is always an adjustment period . . . and as long as you both understand your affection for each other, things will work themselves out." She took Eugenia's hand into hers. "You have told him of your affection, have you not?"

"But Auntie, that is so . . . unladylike."

"And you have never behaved unladylike before?" Aunt Rose regarded her niece from the corner of her eye.

Eugenia had hoped she hadn't seen or heard of those instances. But now she could see she had been clearly mistaken.

"You're a duchess, Genie!" Aunt Rose reprimanded

her in a stern tone. "You have a position in Society. Do not allow your husband to ignore you!"

"Edmund does not ignore me—completely," she said in weak protest. It had been the truth up until this last week. "He's very considerate and attentive . . . when we are together in public."

Aunt Rose leveled a stern gaze at her niece. One that pinned Eugenia's back to her chair and held her immobile for a good minute.

"If he were so attentive, he'd be here spreading jam on your morning toast instead of sitting at Carlton House watching the Prince Regent have his whiskers scraped."

Eugenia hated to admit it but Aunt Rose had never been more correct.

Edmund had not returned to 17 Hanover Square by 6 that evening. Eugenia had waited for hours, hoping for his arrival. She climbed the stairs and heard muffled noises coming from the room next to hers . . . his room. The drag of drawers being drawn opened and firmly closed could be heard though the wall.

Eugenia's heart leaped when she realized it was him. Edmund had returned home. She hadn't thought their confrontation would come this soon but she would not pass up the opportunity. She would take her aunt's advice and tell him she loved him and insist they remain married.

Opening the adjoining doors to their rooms, she

was shocked to find not Edmund, but his valet, Travers.

"What are you doing?" she asked. Eugenia took in the stack of shirts and folded waistcoats the valet had removed from the clothespress.

"His Grace has sent for his evening clothes. He is dining at the club and plans to meet you at Lady Jersey's. I would have informed Your Grace as soon as I had carried out His Grace's request."

"No, it's all right, Travers." But it wasn't all right. Eugenia felt heartbroken.

Travers finished gathering what he needed and left, leaving her alone, standing between the rooms.

Her room was bright and cheerful with flowered wallpaper in pastel colors. In contrast, Edmund's room had damask drapes, two huge oil paintings, and dark paneling. Carved furniture lined the walls while a heavy four-poster bed occupied the center of the enormous room. It looked so much like him, dark and intimidating, a man she understood very little.

Eugenia was very mindful that tonight every little action the new Duke and Duchess of Rothford made would be watched and scrutinized. She would demonstrate, not only to the guests, but to Edmund that she had completely accepted, and would embrace, her new position.

She chose from the selection of the Rothford jewels carefully. Nothing too ostentatious. A simple diamond necklace and matching earbobs to adorn the blue beaded dress she had chosen to wear. Eugenia considered that her first step. Now for the second.

In light of Edmund's absence, Aunt Rose accompanied her to Lady Jersey's. Her aunt's presence, and support, meant more to Eugenia than she could ever say. Once she arrived, Eugenia would find a way . . . somehow . . . in a secluded corner of the ballroom, out on the dance floor, she wasn't sure where but before this night was over, she would find a way to confess that she, the Duchess of Rothford, was in love with her duke.

Lady Jersey welcomed Aunt Rose and Eugenia in the art room. "Mrs. Templeton, it has been an age!"

"Has it been, really? I thought it only this last Season," Aunt Rose expressed with sigh. "And with me is—"

"My duchess—" Edmund's familiar voice interceded and he stepped between them. "May I make known to you Lady Jersey. This is my wife, Eugenia, Duchess of Rothford."

Lady Jersey gasped and dipped into a bow. "Your Grace, it is an exceptional honor."

Eugenia felt stiff and perhaps a bit awkward to be greeted in such a way. "How do you do, Lady Jersey?"

What struck Eugenia the most odd was how Edmund acted toward her. Not as if he were glad to see her and not as though he had not seen her in nearly two days. He had completely ignored the days' separation as if he cared not a fig for her.

Eugenia was introduced to the other fashionable members of Society. It was not too soon until she began to believe in the importance of her new role as duchess herself. And all of it made easier when Edmund stood by her side.

Aunt Rose whispered to Eugenia that she was off to the card room. That may have been true, she was exceedingly fond of cards, but this time Eugenia suspected her aunt wanted to leave her alone with Edmund.

Alone—with the two hundred other guests.

She and Edmund continued down to the large room until they came upon the gallery, brightly lit with oil lamps mounted along the walls, where the dancing took place.

Soon after their arrival, Lady Jersey singled Eugenia for conversation. Edmund excused himself to have a word with a gentleman across the room.

"When Thomas Mallick was Duke of Rothford," Lady Jersey began, "there was not one young lady who could hold his attention. Now, with *Edmund's* return, no one has even had a chance to see him before you two were married."

Eugenia stared at Edmund. She knew how a young female would be attracted to him. Not his wealth or title, but *him* as a man.

At first glance, he appeared tall, dark, and quite

handsome. Upon inspecting his dress one noticed his pristine, intricately tied cravat and his gold threaded waistcoat were finished off with a magnificently tailored Weston coat stretching across his broad shoulders and tapering down to his trim waist. His knee breeches covered his shapely legs and dark satin pumps finished off his evening dress.

After all, he was *her* husband. Those women had a right to be envious. He was kind, thoughtful, and, if she would have given him half a chance, no doubt he would prove loving.

Edmund turned, caught sight of his wife's close inspection, and winked.

A rotation of guests left Eugenia to stand with Mrs. Penshurst, Penelope, and her parents, Lord and Lady Coddington. Moments later, Edmund crossed the room to join them.

"It is so very odd," Mrs. Penshurst went on. "Somehow I thought you married *Thomas* Mallick." She checked Eugenia's face for a reaction. "Well, that can't be, of course. If you're the duchess, you must be married to Edmund here." She thumped her folded fan on the breast of his coat and gave a giddy trill of contrived laughter. "It only stands to reason, doesn't it?"

"Exactly how long have you been back, Your Grace?" Lady Coddington inquired.

An unfettered smile spread across Edmund's face. "Long enough to find my duchess." He sent Eugenia an adoring glance.

"Stole her right from under Thomas' nose, didn't you? Along with his title, I might add," Lord Coddington blustered and nearly choked while laughing.

"Shouldn't speak ill of the dead, Coddington," Lady Coddington scolded. "It was horrible, wasn't it? Of course, I heard your brother died in a terrible accident, soon after you married, was it not, Your Grace?"

"I don't think the details should be repeated. It's not meant for a lady's ear." Edmund should have been in deep mourning but with his extended absence and somewhat questionable marriage, Society seemed to turn a blind eye to his recent family tragedy.

"My, oh my!" Lady Coddington nearly burst at the suggestive nature of the news.

From this point Eugenia found the way Lady Coddington carried on to be abominable. She tried every ploy, technique, and bribe to pry those details out of Edmund. When that didn't work, she turned to Eugenia.

"You were there, weren't you, dear? It must have been horrid, simply horrid!" She brought the tip of her closed fan to her lips to cover her apparent shock.

"Mother, please!" Penelope squealed.

"I'm sorry to disturb you, ladies. My wife has promised me this set." Edmund ushered Eugenia away from the gathering to the dance floor.

My wife . . . Eugenia adored the sound of those words. The way he said them filled her with such pride and longing. She did not know how much longer she could wait to tell him of her true feelings, of the great affection she held for him.

Edmund led her to the dance floor for a waltz. His strong hand around her waist held her near. She warmed as he drew her close. Eugenia wanted to feel that delicious tingle he'd always sent through her when he held her near.

"Closer, my dear," he whispered.

Eugenia's heart fluttered madly, he wanted to be as close to her just as she did to him.

"I wish to speak to you."

Talk? He only wanted to talk to her?

"And I do not want to be overheard."

Disappointed, Eugenia leaned toward him and felt his warm breath against her cheek.

"I do not wish to encourage talk of Franz or events of Thomas' demise."

"How can we possibly avoid it?" Eugenia thought it only natural for others to be curious. "Cynthia and Penelope have told me Franz's interpretation of our elopement. How you abducted me, and—"

"I never said it was me. *Franz* told them it was Rothford." A brief look of confusion crossed his face. "They must have assumed that . . ."

"I suppose I cannot blame you for their embellishments to your tale." Eugenia understood that it was, after all, a matter of interpretation.

"Thank you. I appreciate not having that last bit

set in my plate." There was a bright spark in his dark eyes and he smiled.

It seemed as if it had been an age since he had smiled at her. Grateful that she could rely on him to hold her as they danced, Eugenia felt her arms and knees weaken as she melted in his arms. It felt wonderful.

Eugenia was just about to tell him, right there on the dance floor before everyone, what a fool she had been and how much she loved him.

Then the music stopped and he released her. Eugenia staggered out of his arms, her legs were barely strong enough to keep her from collapsing.

"Shall we get some refreshment, my dear? You look absolutely flushed."

She could well imagine. Edmund headed off to find the lemonade. Eugenia dropped her fan open, cooling herself, pleased that they had progressed to speaking terms.

What could she manage in a roomful of people? Then Eugenia considered a moment and thought . . . Why not take a page from Aunt Rose's book and simply leave because it was the very thing she wished to do?

A few minutes later, Edmund returned to Eugenia's side with a glass. She sipped the lemonade then suggested in the sweetest tone she could manage, "Don't you think we should be leaving?"

"If that is what you wish, my dear," he answered. "Why don't you collect your aunt and we'll be off. I'll accompany the two of you home before heading out for the clubs." He raised her gloved hand to his lips, without even kissing it, and sauntered off to make arrangements for their departure.

Off to the clubs! Eugenia grew angrier and angrier by the minute. She strode into the card room and up to the table where her aunt sat.

"Are you ready to go home, Auntie?" Her aunt's presence in the carriage would ensure His Grace's safety in Eugenia's temper. She would not be tempted to throttle her husband during their long journey home.

"No, no, my dear, you go on ahead. A game of Whist is about to begin. I can manage a ride home." She waved her niece away with an ace of diamonds.

Of all the times Aunt Rose decided to stay, it would have to be this night. Then it occurred to Eugenia that her aunt's success in Society must have been knowing when to remain and when to leave early.

Eugenia stepped outside the card room and spotted Edmund loitering about the foyer. She snapped her fan shut in outrage. She would tolerate his ignoring her no longer.

She loved him, loved him desperately, and still had not managed to tell him. Once they arrived home he would leave her to be alone again.

They would not depart from this residence until Eugenia had her say. She caught up with him at the front door before he retrieved his outerwear and tapped him smartly on the shoulder with her closed fan.

"I must speak to you, Your Grace." She kept her address formal, indicating the seriousness of her intent.

He motioned for her to step down the hallway where they stepped into a small parlor. Edmund momentarily lagged behind and spoke to a footman.

Inside the room, a fire burned in the hearth, directing Eugenia's path. In fact, she found herself pacing the floor, spinning her fan around her wrist. Not only had she nearly worn out her satin slippers, she may have ruined the carpet beneath her feet as well.

Stepping through the doorway, Edmund held a branch of candles and set it on a round table for additional illumination.

"You wish to say something to me, Madam?" He sounded equally as cool as she had been but his manner was far more relaxed.

Now that they stood here, Eugenia was not sure how she would begin. She had not been alone with him for days. If she could not see his expression, perhaps he could not see hers. She hoped the darkened room would mask the discomfort of her admission.

"I wish you were not going out tonight." Her earlier anger and present fear turned to sadness, which overtook her. Eugenia was certain she'd be reduced to a watering pot if he should address her in a disagreeable manner.

"Excuse me?" He leaned toward her, tilting his head to hear what she had to say. "What was that you said?"

"I said . . ." She cleared her throat and repeated, trying to sound steady. "I wish you would not go out tonight."

"Oh," he said simply. "And why is that?"

"By the end of this night I had hoped to tell you of my feelings and how I wish to remain your wife."

"Married . . . and be my duchess?" he whispered in an exhaled breath.

"I do. I would like that above all things." Eugenia nodded, swallowed hard, and waited for his response. After her talk with Aunt Rose, Eugenia could be honest and tell him of her affection.

"My mind is quite made up. I have always thought of you in the highest regard and with great affection." Eugenia gazed up at him. "Actually . . . I believe I have had these feelings for a very long time as you pointed out to me weeks ago. However, it has been only very recently have I come to learn that. I'm being silly and quite contrary, aren't I?"

"You're not silly at all." A smile lit up his face and she could see he was working at keeping his composure. "My heart, my dearest, you know of my love. I have always loved you."

Eugenia knew he loved her, ever since their time in Brighton, ever since he was Franz.

"Your aunt Rose, Mrs. Templeton, persuaded me

that if I should retreat, allow you some time to ponder our predicament, that you should come 'round to the right way of it."

Aunt Rose had suggested . . . *she* had intervened? Eugenia was not entirely pleased that her aunt had interfered in her personal affairs, more specifically, in her marriage. To advise her niece was one thing, but her niece's husband . . .

Edmund fumbled at the pocket of his vest and pulled out something so small it fit in the palm of his hand. Eugenia could not imagine what it was.

"I have a . . ." He glanced at his fingers, fumbling together, demonstrating his nervousness. "I had hoped . . . That is, if you truly loved me then . . . perhaps we might . . ."

Edmund held up a simple gold band for her to see. "Will you marry me?"

Eugenia blinked up at him, finding his reply quite unexpected. "I beg your pardon?"

His voice was calm, although he might have felt nervous, but his manner was most sincere when he took her trembling hand. "I haven't had the chance to ask you if you would do me the honor of becoming *my* wife."

"But we are already married," Eugenia pointed out.

"Our marriage is a legal mishap that should not have occurred. You nor I had any say in the matter even though it was what I desired. I do not believe you would have ever consented to wed me."

He pressed a kiss on the back of her hand, taking his time, doing so slowly, tenderly, and ever so lovingly.

"I thought you might like to be asked. I should think every young lady would want the choice of saying yes . . . or no. Would you do me the honor, Genie?" He looked deep into her eyes and waited.

Eugenia found that she, quite shamelessly, returned his gaze. "It is kind of you to ask." She felt the moment awkward and did not really know what to say next. Perhaps he was correct in thinking she had been adverse to them being married because she had no say in the matter.

She took a step back, away from him. "I suppose I might accept if I felt assured that you would not neglect your husbandly duties."

His eyes widened and he replied, "Don't you mean, my husbandly *rights*?"

"No. Since we are married, I expect my husband to behave in a certain way, and it is your *duty* to do so." Eugenia meant every word.

"Oh, sweet, Genie, you're such an original! Only you could see it that way." He laughed. "You are as enchanting as the first time I met you." His broad smile somehow grew broader. "You stuck that adorable little nose up at me."

"I did no such thing." Eugenia tried to recall exactly when that might have happened.

"It was when I was Franz," he reminded her.

"I never stuck my nose up at Franz," she pouted. Not that he could have seen anyway. It had taken her a bit of time but she did come to see his true nature.

"And I loved you for it!" he laughed.

"You did?" Eugenia wondered how he could have found her behavior in any way charming.

"You too, came to my rescue."

Eugenia could not imagine to what he was referring.

"How many times had you protected Herr Mueller from the poisonous barbs of Lady Penelope?" Edmund traced a line with his fingers along her shoulder. "You're vastly imaginative, totally impulsive, and utterly irresistible!"

"And you don't mind?" She felt a bit self-conscious about the string of multisyllabic adjectives it took to describe her.

"Not in the least."

"And as to being married"—she blinked up at him—"are we? Truly?"

"I believe our situation is no worse than saying vows over an anvil. If it is your wish that we should stand up in St. George's before all of London, we shall do so. You'll look magnificent in your simple white silk gown with a touch of lace. The church will be filled with the bountiful floral contents of ten hothouses worth of peonies. And an enormous, superbly lavish breakfast would follow."

Eugenia's eyes widened as he outlined the wedding

of her dreams. "How did you know that's what I'd always wanted?"

"I was there, *Liebling*, do you not remember? We spent much time together weaving fanciful dreams!"

He had always been there . . . as Franz Mueller the musician and as her brave, handsome duke . . . watching her, protecting her, loving her.

"Are you sure you will be able to leave the life of an Austrian musician behind and take your rightful place as the new duke? It sounds as if you miss Franz."

"I envy him because you were his steadfast friend. But with you by my side, dearest Eugenia, I can face anything." He held the gold band for her between his thumb and index finger, its reflection winked in the fire light.

"And I would not want to be anywhere else." She smiled and slid her finger through the wedding band.

"Being married to you will be a joy beyond compare. You are the very best thing about returning to my old life." Edmund pulled Eugenia into his arms to kiss her. "Let our duet begin!"

FIC
MARKS

Marks, Shirley.

Lady Eugenia's
  holiday.

$23.95

DATE			

28
Day
Loan

BAKER & TAYLOR